Get On Point

By: Devon Wilfoung

First print 2016 Oct

This is a book of fiction. Any references or similarities to actual events, real people, or real locations are intended to give the novel a sense of reality. Any similarity to other names, characters, places and incidents are entirely coincidental.

ISBN-13:978-
ISBN-10:

Allison S.T. Publications LLC.
P.O. BOX xxx GLENDALE. MD xxxxx

Email: Allison S.T. Publications@
Editing by: Eric Gardner/Intrepid Publications LLC
Written by: Devon Wilfoung co-CEO, Allison ST Publications LLC.

Publisher: Devon Wilfoung co-CEO, Allison ST Publications LLC.
Alekia watts co-CEO, Allison ST Publications LLC

Cover Design: Crystell Publications
Book Productions: Crystell Publications
We Help You Self Publish Your Book
(405)414-3991

ACKNOWLEDGMENTS

I would like to give a very special thanks to everyone who gave a helping hand to make this book so memorable. Avonia Wilfoung, Crystell Perkins, J-Sun Love, Tiffany Steele, Desiree Dockery, Toriano Natash, Vick Qwest, Charles Barber, Whodie, Gregory Worsley, Vernon, Grant, Chevy Boy.

Thank you all for your help. I also want to dedicate this book to the city of High Point, NC. I hope everyone enjoys it. I also want to spread love and prayer throughout the city. There was so many senseless killings and families that went through so much grief. I only hope that we will act responsibly and be our brother's and sister's keepers. My condolences to the families that lost a loved one. If you lost a loved one sign their name ________________
In Loving Memory.

The name I filled in was my cousin, Gilbert Barber. He inspired this book. He use to always tell the crew to Get On Point. The saying means to always be on your P's and Q's. Never slip, never give up. And always strive to be the best. R.I.P. Anytime I want to hear a story about you I just go to Jessie Barber, Calvert Butch Stewart, Marcus, Art, Grandma, Rashawn or Atari. The family as well as friends will always miss you!
And to my Aunt Camilia! I know you're in a better place. Going to miss you beautiful. Tell TY we said hi, and Aunt Barber, Grandma Babe, Aunt Cat, Randy Lagrand, Dennis! I know you told me and the family to watch out for Aaron. We will my Angel! That's what family is for. Also missing A-Dog and Jahaun! O'Brian Johnson, Mytra Bullet, Jacob Walker Derek Brown, Dontae Gilmore and Keith Watson.

Chapter 1

"Boom, boom! "

Around here only the strong survived. To live until you were twenty-three was over achieving. The reason for the shots being fired. We caught a nigga who thought just because he had a girl who lived in our projects that that gave him permission to set up shop. That was definitely a no-no. His ass wouldn't live to see tomorrow.

"Caught this bitch ass nigga selling work in apartment 24-A." Gun's tossed the intruder on the roof top and stomped
him with his size 12 Timberland boots. "Is you crazy mother-fucker!" asked Gun's, sucker punching the intruder. His face went one direction and blood from his mouth flew the other. "Thought we wouldn't find out?" Gun's spat in the intruders face. "Cock- sucker." Gun's was a real nigga. Ever since he had got robbed at gun point by two gorgeous strippers, he punished everyone like they had something to do with it. Gun's was known for busting his gun and considered a lunatic, but on the flip side of things known to get distracted when it came to bitch's with pretty faces and

phat ass's.

"Kill that nigga," Peace gave the command and his Q-Infinity gang started busting shots. Peace made his way from the roof top as shots rang out. That would teach mother-fuckers not to disrespect him and his Q-Infinity clique. If a nigga made a dollar and wasn't from their projects then he had to pay with his life.

Peace took the staircase down to his girl Trish's apartment on the eighth floor, and used his key to get in. As usual she was getting ready to hit the club. This bothered him since she was pregnant with his seed. Trish was everything a hustler could dream of.

She was 5ft6, 140 pounds with a slim waist, thick hips, round ass and she sort of looked like the female MC, Trina. Peace walked up behind Trish and kissed the nape of her neck as she fixed her hair. Where you think you going?" he asked.

She turned to face him. She grabbed her beer and took a sip. "Out ."

"You know you can't be drinking that shit now that you having my seed." He pulled her against him and took the drink out of her hand.

He didn't have a clue. She looked at him like he was crazy. "You a joke." She belittled him. "Do you think I would actually have a kid by you?" she spat. "You a hoe. Plus you won't live to see twenty four. The way you living you'll be dead or either locked up, shot up, or stabbed the fuck up. Plus you don't know the first thing about raising a child. "

She turned back toward the mirror and started back

fixing her hair like she didn't just have an abortion.

He tried to think rational and take in what she just said. He wanted to choke slam Trish' s dumb-ass. Sometimes he wanted to kill this stupid bitch. He took a deep breath so he wouldn't fly off the handle. "So you telling me you had another abortion?"

"Yeah," She snapped. "That's what I'm saying, you should learn to wrap that shit up. I need some money to go out with." She held out her hand. "I spent the last bit of money I had on the abortion."

Be strong, Peace told hisself. "Fuck you bitch! " He left out of Trish's crib slamming the door hard as fuck. Talk about anger, He flew down the stairs two at a time and made his way to his Range Rover. He felt like the walls of Babylon was falling down on him. He sat in his SUV and then pulled off. All he could do was ask God why. Trish was always doing some stupid ass shit. He looked at his cell that was going off.

"Yo, what's good?"

"You tell me, man. I know you gon' be at the Sugar Shack tonight. You know you gotta show your face and let everyone know that Q-infinity in the place to be," said Justice, Peace's ace-boon-coon.

"Most definitely," said Peace. "One." He replied as he hung up. He drove through the city of High Point. Juanita Hills, J.C. Morgan, Carson Stout, Farmington, and Daniel Brooks. High Point was the furniture capital of the world. Furniture wasn't the only thing that was going on in High Point, N.C. High Point was one of the main cities for coke and heroin. The crime rate was in such a high state, that the

F.E.D.S. would often come through and lock up the big time drug lords and leave the small fish to finish were the big time hustlers left off. Peace glanced out the window as he drove, and looked at what the city had become. There was only a couple ways out the ghetto as he knew, death or the motherfucking jail house. He chose neither even though the odds were stacked up against him. He stared down at his platinum chain and traced his hand across his Jesus piece and asked himself, "God why does my life have to be like this."

Peace parked his Range Rover in the parking garage where he lived and went into his studio flat. He tossed his keys on the sofa and went to take a much needed shower. Afterwards he got dressed, fed his pitbull pup, Gambino. Then left for the club.

When he reached the club shit was bumper to bumper, he pulled in front of the club and parked at his reserved parking space. He had one thing on his mind and that was to find something to take his mind off of Trish and his unborn child.

"Yo. We been waiting all night for you," said Bear. head of security as Peace got out of his Range Rover. "Let me get you in the club,"

Sometimes it paid to be a part owner of an what's happening club. Just a few things money could do, "Good look," Peace said to Bear.

"No problem, bossman," Bear left and went to go attend the front door.

***

Yolanda, a.k.a. Yo-Yo, Sugar Sweet and Cherry walked through the crowd, all eyes were on their pretty eyes and sexy thighs. Yolanda and her girls used their gorgeous looks and curvaceous assets to rob big time hustlers. Their motto was, fuck niggas get money." They were dressed to kill. Yolanda had on a black Chanel dress and heels. Sugar Sweet wore black bootie heels and off the shoulder dress by DKNY; that revealed her erect nipples. There was no shame in her game. She was looking to set a nigga up.

Cherry wore a super duper short dress that showcased her hourglass figure. After finally paying their entrance fee and getting inside of the club, they set out to find a couple of ballers to rob for the night. Sugar Sweet found her first victim, "Girl. Look over there. Ten o'clock," she tilted her head toward a guy chilling with his friends. He had on an iced out necklace that appeared to be very costly, "see you all later, "Sugar responded by making her way over to the guy with the heavy bling on.

"She is so crazy," declared Yolonda to Cherry, "Cherry," she spent around after no reply and bumped into a sexy roughneck kind of brother. He was wearing fatigues and Tim boots.

"Oh, I'm so sorry,' she said as his drink splatter all over him.

"I can be so clumsy sometimes," she tried wiping his shirt as if she had super powers, "can I buy you something else to drink," she asked after seeing it was no use of her trying to wipe his shirt off, the damage was already done. His shirt was pretty much ruined.

Peace wiped his shirt off and looked at shorty. If she

wasn't so fine he probably would've smacked fire out of her.

"Only if you have a drink with me," he stared at her thinking how much she resembled the actress Sanaa Lathan.

The way he was looking at her was almost as if he was peering into her soul. She didn't know what it was about him that sent chills through her body? Normally she had zero tolerance for conversation while handling business, but this was a rare occasion, "I guess one drink wouldn't hurt. What would you care to have,"

"Thug Passion," He told her.

"Me too. One of my favorite drinks of all time," she smiled thinking about how much he reminded her of the rap artist Nas, "Let's go over to the bar," she lead the way. She could feel his eyes on her. She turned back and her thoughts were confirmed. He was definitely checking her out, "two cups of thug passion, please," she cited to the bartender.

"Twenty eight bucks," replied the Bartender.

Yolanda paid the bartender and passed her secret admire his drink, What. What's up," She glared at him. The way he was checking her out had her nervous, and not to mention damp! She wanted to just take him home and climb on top of his fine ass.

"I just ain't use to a woman doing shit for me. Thanks, yo," he took a sip of his drink.

"Maybe it's the type of women you're dealing with," she shot back.

"Maybe you're right," he took a sip from his drink and

asked, "You live around here,"

She giggled, "yes," she could see that he wanted her almost as bad as she wanted him.

"Funny I have never saw you around," he thought that to be odd since he knew damn near everyone from his hometown.

"I keep my business out the streets," she stated , "I'm not your ordinary girl. " She replied, taking a sip of her drink.

"Bartender." He motioned over. "Let me and the lovely lady get another drink on the house," said Peace.

Yolonda could tell that he was a man of power and she had to admit that she was impressed.

"What's your name, and most important. Before we go any further?" he asked as the bartender returned with the drinks. "Do you have a man?" It's not like he cared, but still had to ask to make sure.

She finished her first drink and grabbed the one the bartender had sat down on the counter. "You kinda getting personal. Here I am buying you a drink and you hitting me with all these questions. Damn," she spat.

He laughed. "Check it, ma. I'ma get at you cause I got some business to take care of. Maybe if you still here I'll get at you." Peace stepped off as his crew approached.

"Get to stepping then. I don't need you." She sucked her teeth pissed off he just pushed her to the side. He wasn t her type anyway. She thought as he dapped his boys up.

After the club closed, Yolonda and her girls stood outside the club scoping out who they were going to rob. Yolonda glimpsed at the guy who said he was gonna get at her but never did. The one who pushed her to the side. She stared at a guy staggering with a trench coat opening up his jacket clutching onto a gun.

"Look out!" she screamed.

"What the fuck shorty talking about?" He took one look at the screw faced nigga with the chip on his shoulder and reached for his Desert Eagle. "Boom, boom, boom. " Peace let shots rip. He hit his victim three times and watched as the body slumped to the ground.

"Yo, give me your gun." Bear took the gun from Peace and helped him to his ride. "Get outta here. "

Peace burned out. He was mad as shit. All the niggas he was with but yet and still, a bitch he hardly knew had been the only one on point.

His heart was racing like the Daytona 500. He went to the safest place he knew, Irving Projects. He parked and went inside to one of his working spots. His mind was wondering, still trying to figure out who tried to murk him. Could it be some out of town nigga? Maybe it was the young nigga they killed on the roof, people trying to retaliate. Whoever it was gonna feel it.

***

"Girl, who was that nigga? He was fine! You saved his life. His ass would've been dead if he hadn't been so focused on your short ass dress," Cherry teased. "He better be glad
he had his gun or else his ass would've been one dead

nigga. He must be a big time nigga if someone tried to take his life like that," said Cherry to Yolonda.

"I don't know. All I know is I spilled a drink on his shirt and never did get his name," said Yolonda.

"You ain't get his name and number how fine he was?" asked Sugar.

"He was cocky, plus he didn't look like he had money like that," Yolonda shot back.

"He sure looked like he had money to me. Let me find out that nigga making you soft. You can't think with your legs. Think about that Range Rover he was pushing. " Sugar dropped some wisdom on her girl.

Yolonda knew her girl was only looking out for her, but she wanted what she wanted and that's just the way it was.

CHAPTER 2

"Get the fuck on the ground. Don't move or make a sound. First one act up the first one catching a cap. Take this rope and tie his sorry ass up," the gunman screamed at Cherry.

She cried and played her role. "Don't kill us. Please don't kill us! Shawn. Tell them where the money is, baby before they kill us."

"Fuck them," Shawn yelled like he was tough as Cherry tied his arms up tight with rope.

"Please, Shawn! They gonna kill us." Tears slid down Cherry's face.

"Shut up bitch and stop all that damn crying before I kill you," the female gunman said before tossing Cherry to the ground and pressing the gun up to her head.

"Kill her," said the other gunman.

"No! no. Hold up," said Shawn.

"Give up the shit and you and your bitch can get back to doing your thing, little man." The female gunman looked down at his button sized dick and laughed.

"Alright," said Shawn. He had never been so humiliated in his life. "You promise to let me go?" asked Shawn.

"What about me, Shawn?" asked Cherry in tears.

"Fuck you bitch," said Shawn thinking about his own ass.

"Yeah, I promise to let you go scott free," said one of the female gunmen.

"Upstairs in the closet to the left," he said hoping that he lived another day.

"Go check that, sweetie," Yolonda said to Sugar Sweet.

Sugar Sweet came back with a large pillowcase of money and drugs. "Yep, looks like we hit the jackpot."

"What we gonna do with him?" asked Cherry as she tossed on her clothes.

"You bitch! " spat Shawn.

"Boom, boom." "I had my fingers crossed asshole," Yolonda said killing for the first time. This was her first major lick and she didn't want the shit leading back to them.

"What the fuck is wrong with you? Why the fuck you kill him for? Let's get out of here before the cops come," Cherry snapped.

They all left out the house never looking back. They got to the tinted up van they hid in the cut and changed clothes. They trashed the clothes used for the heist, then they all split up and met back at Sugar's house. There they divided seventy-five thousand and a little over two kilos of powder. This was a good lick, but their next involved more risk.

***

"Ring, ring." "Who the hell is that?" Showtime asked Unity.

"I don't know," said Unity snatching open the door. His mouth dropped as he stared at the sexy sister at the door.

"Sup, shorty? You lost? I think you got the wrong address."

"Nope. This is 1214 Kennedy Street, isn't it?" said Sugar as she stepped into the small duplex.

"Yeah, but! " Unity said speechless.

She let her coat fall to the floor exposing her half naked body. All she had on was a bra and a G-string. "Your boss told me to come by and reward y all for all your good work. All work and no play can drive a man insane."

"I heard that shorty." Showtime got up and stopped playing the video game.

Sugar Sweet danced to the Freeway album as it bumped through the speakers . She gave them a show they would never forget. They were so busy watching her bend over that they didn't notice the figures creeping in. She picked up the money they were tossing around and smiled. She slightly slid her G-Sting to the side revealing her well shaven vagina.

"Oh shit!" Unity said excited. He groped his dick and asked, "How much to fuck?"

"Your life." Sugar pulled a twenty-five caliber from her knee high boots. "Hands up so I can see them. Now! " she demanded.

"Be good and do whatever mommie tells you to do." Some niggas just couldn't stand the fact that a woman was sticking their ass the fuck up. "Sit tight until Mommie gets back." Sugar left to go search for the money and product, while Yolonda and Cherry held the two thugs at gun point. Sugar returned with a shit load of money and coke. "Let's go."

"Not until we kill these niggas first," said Yolonda.

"What?" Sugar asked somewhat surprised. "That wasn't part of the plan," she said.

Unity used the distraction to reach into his pocket for his gun. "Bitch!" He yelled as he pulled it out.

"Boom, boom, boom." The Tech let loose." Cherry stood over the motionless body with a smoking gun.

"What about him?" Yo-Yo asked looking at Showtime. "Boom!" Sugar killed him on the spot with her .25 and they broke out.

CHAPTER 3

"The reason I called this meeting," Peace took a puff from his blunt and proceeded, "Is because lately niggas been slipping.

We the largest projects and still got niggas disrespecting us like crazy. Two of our spots got hit in the last month, plus I got niggas try'na take my fucking head off. No more of this shit!" Peace grilled every member in his clique to let them know he was dead serious. Y'all need to get on point," Peace said before leaving the meeting and going out onto the balcony to get some fresh air. As he puffed on some Purple

Haze rolled in an Optimo blunt, Crook joined him.

"Yo, you alright?" asked Crook. "What's on your mind?"

"Just try'na make some sense out of all this shit. Like why the fuck the spots keep getting ran up in. We can't have niggas thinking we soft. If we keep this up we gonna end up in the poor house," Peace stressed.

"Right. Ain't nothing soft about Q-Infinity. " Crook took the blunt Peace gave him.

He took a tote of the Haze and exhaled. "Yo, Justice told me you probably wouldn't be down, but we about to rob them niggas in Daniel Brook Projects. I think they robbed and killed Showtime and Unity. The way I see it, we get them before they get us," declared Crook.

Peace rubbed his face as he thought about the situation. "What's the plan?"

Crook explained, "We hit them niggas, split the money and then hit our favorite strip club, Cabaret."

***

They wasted no time applying the pressure to the niggas in Daniel Brooks. Crook kicked the door from off the hinges at the spot they were robbing. Justice and Peace entered with their semi-automatics. Once inside they made everyone get on the floor.

"One false move and I'm letting it go," Peace responded by showcasing his AK- 47 tightly, ready to murder anything breathing too hard.

"Make this shit easy and keep living." Peace stated as he watched everyone as Justice and Crook patted the motherfuckers down, taking their money, coke, and personal stashes. Justice left and went in the backroom. He returned with two duffle bags. "Let's be out," said Just.

Peace was so busy watching the motherfuckers on the ground that he failed to see the gun that was pressed to the back of his head.

"Not so fast. Drop those guns or he dies," The female gunman said to everyone. When they placed their guns down she nodded to Sugar. "Go get those bags." Sugar did like Yolanda asked her and returned with the two duffle bags. "Looks like we hit the jackpot," Assured Sugar, clutching what appeared to be a wealthy heist.

"Some hoe's. You gotta be kidding me." Peace whipped around and got a good look at the female gunman behind the wig and ski-mask. "Can I buy you a drink?" he recognized her as the shorty who spilled the drink on him at the club.

"You can't afford it sloppy." Oh shit! How did he know who she was? Thought Yolanda.

There was no way she could kill him. Not after all the restless nights she had sat up thinking about him.

"Let me see those bags," She announced to Sugar as Cherry watched the door. She took the bag with the money and gave the one with the coke and drugs to him. "Get out of here, and take your school pigeons with you!" She shoved him out the door and watched as he and his entourage ran off into the night.

***

"Damn. A hundred and ninety- five thousand. That was our best lick ever. Yolonda acknowledged. She began waving stacks in Sugar's face.

Sugar wasn't too pleased, she commented. "Would've been."

"Why you upset," questioned Yolonda.

"You don't know? You gave away half of our earnings. I could've let my boo flip that. You thinking with your legs and you gonna be all fucked up off of a nigga like you was with Jo-Jo."

Jo-Jo was Yolonda's ex. She hadn't heard from him over two years. Hearing his name brung forth a lot of bad memories. She could remember once upon a time when there was nothing she wouldn't have done for Her sorry excuse for an Ex. She use to traffic his drugs, and as soon as he blew up, he did what? Left her for the next bitch. She hadn't heard from Jo-Jo, but last she had heard, he was somewhere in Raleigh, NC. Doing his thing.

"Why did you have to go there? He knew who I was and I was kind of jocking that cute ass nigga." Stated Yolanda. Speaking about the recent heist in which she gave away half the caper.

"You need to hear it. You could've got us killed. Just because you jocking a nigga don't mean you have to let him walk away with that type of money," declared Sugar.

"Cherry, do you think I was wrong," Yolanda asked.

"Don't put me in the middle of you alls squabble." Cherry answered as she went right back to recounting money.

CHAPTER 4

"We rob these niggas and got everybody on the ground when Mr. Ain't On Point Peace let some bitch's rob us. This nigga the joke of the city right now. He don't need no gun. Can I buy you a drink?'" Crook did his best Peace impersonation. "The bitch about to kill us and you asking about a drink. Thirsty ass nigga. Gun's ain't got shit on you. I'm taking him with me next time. He can resist them ho's better than you," said Crook. Justice and the rest of the crew cried with laughter.

"Yeah, but at least that bitch gave us half the lick and let us walk out with a quarter million in drugs. Gun's ain't that damn sexy. I talked my way out of death and saved yall' s ungrateful ass's." As Crook, Justice and the crew continued to laugh, Peace got up from the sofa and decided he wasn't going to be the butt of their jokes any longer.

"I'm out. Yall need to quit talking about yesterday," said Peace.

"You need to check your ho's," said Justice as Peace walked out the door.

Peace made his way through the PJ's and spoke to everyone on his way to the corner store.

"Aaah! Peace. Give me a few dollars and I'll sing you a nice song." Top the town drunk began to snap his fingers to gain a rhythm. "Even when your hustling days are gone she'll still be by your side still holding on. Even when those twenties stop spinning and those gold digging women disappear, she'll still be here. Must be nice! " Top sang what he knew of the Lyfe Jennings track and stopped when he couldn't remember the rest.

"Yo, Don't do that again. That shit was horrible," responded Peace, breaking Top off a twenty dollar bill from his large knot of money. Poor Top. After his girl left him back in the day he had never quite bounced back and had became accustomed to drinking ever since. Peace went into Mr. Fuller on Green Street. The only black owned establishment in the community. He purchased a box of Optimo blunts, a beer, and some scratch off cards. As he scratched from his card a black Mercedes Benz 500 pulled in his path as he crossed the street. He reached for his pistol as the windows began to roll down. "What the fuck are you doing?" He gritted his face into a mean mug. "Trying to get killed."

"No, I been looking for you." Yolanda replied.

Peace calmed his nerves a little, "well, you found me. What you want." He was still salty about shorty and her girls making off with all of the money and making him look like a complete idiot in front of his boys.

She responded. "I don't want to fight. I just want to get to know you. "Get in,"

"Bitch is you crazy," He wanted to know. "I ain't going nowhere with your shiesty ass. I don't fuck wit shiesty motherfuckers."

She could see that he was leery of her. "I promise I'm not trying to rob you. Look. That wasn't meant for you. You just kinda walked into it. My name is Yolanda but my friends call me Yo-Yo for short." She focused her attention on a girl approaching.

"Peace, who is that bitch!" Trish commented as she made her way across the street.

"I'm not leaving until you get in," Yolanda told him. "Is that your girlfriend? She looks pissed the hell of. You better get in or explain to her what you doing all up in my face." She giggled.

"You's a no good, hoe, nigga." Trish hurled her purse at Peace just as he hopped into the car with some bitch.

Yolonda pulled off as Peace took a deep sigh in the passenger side of the car. He looked like he was going through some problems with his girl. Good, she thought to herself. "You like Jaheim?" she asked.

"That nigga ain't never did shit to me," replied Peace still looking back to see if somehow by possible chance that Trish was still following him.

Yolonda flipped the dial on the radio and the Jaheim CD started to play. "You wanna talk about that girl that was chasing you back there?"

"Nope."

She looked over at him and asked, "Don't you owe me something?"

"I don't owe you shit!" he japped.

"Don't be taking what you and your girl got going on out on me, she snapped.

"Watch it shorty," Peace scolded.

"You watch it," she mumbled.

"So, you be out here robbing folks. I didn't know that's how you got down. "

"If they sloppy then I will. You don't have to worry cause I don't stick up petty niggas," she giggled.

Shorty had him in his joint. "If I'm so petty why you checking for me?"

"Oh please! I wasn't checking for you." She lied. "I just want that drink you owe me. I hope you got your chips up cause I forgot my purse." She drove to a nice Italian restaurant in downtown High Point called Valintino's. She parked and they got out and went inside.

If his niggas knew he was out with one of the girls who had made off with their cash they would call him all kind of sucker for love ass niggas. "What you want to eat?" asked Peace.

"Spaghetti," said Yolonda smiling at him for the first time.

"Spaghetti. Bring us a bottle of your finest Chardonnay," he told the waiter. Yolonda was so innocent but yet capable of pulling off a major robbery. "Is your hair real or is it fake like those wigs you and your girls wear?"

"Why don't you pull it and find out," she said being sarcastic.

He tugged her hair with the quickness. "I guess it is your real hair. Your name Yolonda or that the alias you go by?"

She was tired of him trying to play her. "Look.

Everything about me is real ain't nothing fake. Don't knock what I do." She got upset.

"Look," said Peace, "I ain't knocking what you do. But the shit you doing gonna get you hurt. Don't ever try me like that again or else I might have to kill you next time." He paused as the waiter sat their plates down. When he left he added, "Now let that be the last time you pull some shit like that. Next time you won't be so lucky," stated Peace as he tried out the spaghetti.

Who did Peace think he was? She let him stroke his own ego and sat back quietly and ate. After dinner she was feeling a little tipsy from the Chardonnay. "You ready to leave?" she asked Peace.

"If you are ," he replied.

"Yeah. I'm ready. " She got up from the table.

Peace paid the bill and left the waiter a tip. He grabbed the smalls of Yolonda's back and lead her out of Valintino's. Damn, she was falling for Peace all too soon, thought Yolonda as Peace lead her to the car safely. She managed to drive off and handle her drink without crashing. As she drove Peace took off his shirt and she momentarily took her eyes off the road and stared at his stout physique. Boy was he ripped up, she thought. Gosh!

"How long has it been?" he asked.

"What?" she focused back on the road.

"How long has it been since you been fucked right?"

Her mouth dropped. "I don't think that's none of your business."

"Where we going, your place?" He leaned over and kissed her softly across her shoulder.

"No. We can't go to my place," she said as he planted kisses from her shoulder to her neck.

Peace stopped what he was doing. "You said that like you got your man at the spot or something. "

Nope. But Sugar and Cherry were hanging out at her house and if she took Peace to her house then they would have a fucking fit. She decided against that. "I don't have a man, but we can't go to my place."

Peace wondered if shorty was worth the head ache. She had more secrets than a little bit, like what else was he gonna find out about her. "Yo, shoot to my crib. Bust this right, right here. "

"I thought you lived in Irving Projects? This is the wrong way," said Yolanda as she turned like he told her to.

"I do but I don't hustle where I lay my head. " He gave Yolonda the directions to his crib.

Yolonda pulled into the parking garage and parked.

"You corning in?" asked Peace. "You too bent to be driving anyway. "

She said in defense mode, "I'm not drunk. Plus I drove this far and you didn't say nothing. "

Peace leaned over and snatched the keys out of the ignition. "Bring your ass," he said. He waited for Yolonda. They took the elevator. He could tell Yolonda was upset about him taking the keys even though she lead on like she wasn't. He noticed how beautiful she was while they took the elevator. Yolonda was 5ft5, 120 pounds at the most with a caramel brown skin tone and coke bottle figure. Even without make-up she still looked better than most women, thought Peace as the elevator stopped on his floor.

He lead the way to his studio apartment, and used the keys to open the door. Soon as he got the door open Gambino rushed at them. Yolonda took off running as he scooped his pitbull up. "It's only a puppy," he laughed.

"Put him up. He sounds ruthless." She waited for Peace to put the dog in it's cage and then went and took a seat on the sofa.

"I'll be back. " Peace went into the bathroom and took a piss with the door open so he could watch shorty.

"Yolonda got up and started browsing around. She glimpsed at a picture of Peace with his crew, picture of him flossing some of his expensive whips, and one with the girl who threw the purse at him earlier. She walked around and wondered who had decorated Peace's crib, because his shit was laid out. He had wall to wall carpet, a fireplace , and an expensive leather living-room set. She jumped as Peace came back into the living room. She placed her hand over her heart, "you startled me."

Peace exhaled the blunt he had just lit up. He could tell she had been rambling through his shit. "You can look around if you want," He stated what he had already witness her doing.

She snarled at him. "Funny." She took a seat beside him. "So The girl that threw the purse at you when I picked you up? Do you love her? I see you have a picture of her up."

"Trish," He answered, laughing to himself. "We not together anymore. If I loved her do you think you would be over here?"

'That's real, " retorted Yolanda. Made her feel a lot better. "What happened to the two of you?"

"If I answer your question can you answer me this?" He asked.

"Ask me anything," She smiled.

"What happened with you and your man, I mean," He paused. "You too damn sexy not to have no man in your life," He lifted her chin up to see her pretty eyes and face, glancing into her soul.

She smiled, liked being in his presence. "You promise not to laugh if I tell you?"

"Promise," he answered.

"Well, for three whole years I helped hold my man down on the hustle tip. Trafficking his drugs for him, cooking his drugs up, you name it. I was in love with Jo-Jo. And what did he do?" He blew up and started sleeping with every bitch who would give it up. The more money I helped him make the less I saw of him. I finally got tired of his shit and left." She was so embarrassed about her revelation. "You not gonna laugh?" She asked.

"Nah, sorry to hear that," Peace answered with sympathy.

"You're not getting off the hook. I told you so it's your turn. Trish," She inquired.

"Long story. Trish and I were together since we were high school seniors. I was in the streets and she was right behind me. "

"And. The reason yall not together?" asked Yolonda wanting to know more.

Peace hit the blunt and looked at Yolonda as he let out a cloud of smoke. "One too many abortions. "

"How many did she have?" asked Yolonda. She felt bad

for Peace, because he looked like he was really hurt.

"Two."

"Urmn. " She could feel his pain. She wanted to cry with him. Tell him that it would be alright, to tell him he didn't need Trish, that all he needed was someone like her. She took the blunt from Peace and took a puff. They both had been hurt by their significant other. Maybe they were the solution to one anothers problem. She found herself wanting. Out of the pure blue sky she leaned over and kissed Peace slow but passionate. Her hand scanned it's way to his six pack. As he kissed her she kissed him back with the same intensity. He scooped her up from the sofa and took her to his room, where he placed her down at the foot of the bed . His cell rang.

"Don't answer that ." She tried her hardest to get the cell out of his hand. She even wrapped her legs around him so he wouldn t take the call. "Let it ring," she said.

He kissed Yolonda as he got a peek of the screen. "Yo, I gots to get this. This is my boy Just." He slid out of her fierce leg lock. "Yo, Just. Hold up. " He left out the room so shorty wouldn't eaves drop on his conversation.

"Yo, what up?" he asked Just as he stepped in the hallway.

"Man, police just did a sweep. Stay away from the Projects for a couple days. Shit hotter than a mother! I gotta bail out a couple of our guys that got bagged in the sting, but don't worry. I'ma handle everything. One ."

"Damn." Peace rubbed his head after receiving the call from Just. What else could happen. He thought as he went back into his bedroom. Yolanda had kicked off her shoes, got undressed and was passed out on the bed. Peace grabbed an Optimo blunt, a bag of loud reefer and rolled up, then went out on the balcony that overlooked the city and fired up his blunt. He thought about how he and his Q-Infinity clique had managed to come up. Not long ago they were doing whatever for the paper. Stick ups, purse snatching, stealing cars, robbing foreigners and out of towners at the furniture conventions. Those were the days. Now he was twenty- three and the head of the clique. He glimpsed at Yolanda's half naked body, and went and got in bed with her. He wrapped his arms around her tender body and got some sleep.

Yolanda woke up in Peace's embrace. She was so glad he hadn't taken advantage of her. Then again. Was her wishful thinking. She kissed Peace's cheek and rubbed his handsome face before throwing on her clothes and quietly departing.

Peace woke up to an empty bed. No Yolanda. It was like everything that walked into his life walked out. He got up and took a cold shower, brushed his teeth, then got dressed. He tossed on a white tank top, black Polo jeans shorts and brand new Jordans. He left out the crib and hopped into his black Maserati Quattro port. He cruised the city. Hitting up Carson Stout, J.C Morgan, Five Points, Greenstreet, Eastside, Brentwood, Daniel Brooks, Juanita Hills, Cedar and forth, and by Washington Terrace, as he was making his way past Park Street and the Granby area, White Oak, Walnut, he headed toward MLK and was stopped by a police officer. "Shit," He silently uttered as he was pulled over. Lucky for him the cop was only racial profiling and nothing more. They were probably curious to see a black man driving such an extravagant car. "Fuck the police," He mouthed off as he drove off switching lanes on his way to his homeboy, Just house in Emerywood. A predominately white neighborhood. Unlike him, Justice lived life to the fullest. He parked beside Just's Bentley coupe and got out. He walked by a red H2 Hummer, a black Chrysler 300, dark blue Dodge Magnum and white Cadillac Escalade. He made his way to the door and rung the bell.

"You must be Peace?" a sexy cutie asked as she opened the door. "Just has told me so much about you." She let Peace in and lead him to Justice.

This nigga was wild as shit! Peace thought as shorty lead him to a pool. Justice's crib was unbelievable. He had an indoor basketball court, weight room, swimming pool, six bedrooms, three bathrooms, and movie theater. Just was in a small ass float with two hot babes on each arm sipping bubbly.

"What up nigga?" asked Just. "I see you met Goldshay? Take my bro in the guest room and fuck his brains out. That's my bro so make sure he has a great time," he told Goldshay.

That was the thing Peace loved about Justice. He was fair. Guessed that was the reason people called him Just, pondered Peace as he followed Goldshay to the guest room. Looking at her coke figured body he imagined the things he would do to her.

"I hope you have protection," asked Goldshay as she took his hand and lead him to the bed.

"No doubt." Peace sat on the bed as Goldshay got

undressed.

Goldshay was a sexy chocolate complexion, she was tall, and resembled Taral Hicks who played DMX girlfriend in the movie Belly. As her dress fell to the floor, he could see her body clearer. She had nice size tits, long legs, firm hips, and apple shaped ass. He aroused to his feet and pulled the condom out of his pocket, he tore the wrapper with his teeth and applied it on. He spun Goldsay around and plunged into her already moist slit. He stroked hard and repeatedly, thrusting his hips in and out.

"Gosh!" She rubbed her tits as he drove in her with long deep strokes. "Yes, baby. That feels so good," she moaned.

"Oh Gosh! Don't stop!" She begged. "It feels so good! I'm about to cum!" She cried out as he crammed more dick in her, making her feel every inch of him.

He flipped her around and then mounted her. He moved in and out until he became weak and climaxed. He collapsed on top of Goldshay as her body trembled underneath him.

CHAPTER 5

All day I've been thinking about Peace. See. He's the only man who has touched me in two years. "Oh baby," I'm sorry. I won't ever leave like that again. I love you," said Yolonda as she kissed Peace fiercely.

Peace lost his jeans and briefs and stood before Yolonda rock hard. Show me how much you love me."

Yolonda got down on her knees and blessed Peace. He was long as a ruler and thick as a pickle. She kissed his erection, and bobbed her head up and down as she took him inch by inch.

"Gosh you're so big." She slurped as his eyes closed and his head drifted back uncontrollably. She stood to her feet.

"Hit it from the back," she suggested.

"Turn around," He tossed her around and slid into her with no hesitation.

"Bang! Bang! Bang!" Are you going to let someone else get in the freaking bathroom, it's four p.m. and I'm ready to get my shopping on. "Hurry the fuck up." Spat Sugar, walking off mad.

At the mall the trio did a lot of shopping. They bought some cute outfits, purses and expensive heels. Yolonda looked at a Gucci dress she thought she would look good in for Peace. She smiled as she grabbed the dress from off the rack. "I can't wait until he sees me in this!" Yolonda assured herself. After they ate at Elizabeth pizza. Jo-Jo walked up on them out of the pure blue sky.

"What up, boo. I see ain't nothing change." He glimpsed at Yolanda's fat ass. Seemed like she was even thicker now than she was when she was with him, Jo-Jo reflected. "What happened? You get your number changed or something." Seeing her brought back old memories.

Yolonda sucked her teeth and ignored his dumb ass.

"Look, ma. I ain't come over here to talk your head off. I just saw you and thought that I would come and speak."

"Well, you spoke. Good bye! " said Yolonda, dismissing him.

"Damn, shorty. It's like that?" asked Jo-Jo.

"Yeah, it's like that," spat Yolonda.

"Look. I'm only in town for the weekend, and I would really like to see you before I go. How about you and your girls come to the Rap Wars at the Sugar Shack? I got tickets to V. I.P." He pulled out tickets from his pockets and placed them onto their table. "I hope to see you," said Jo-Jo as he walked off.

"Girl. Let me see those tickets. Sugar grabbed the tickets up. "I know we going. I heard that shit is supposed to be off the chain. It's gonna be a whole lot of niggas with money in the place. " Sugar danced in her seat. "I heard the winner of the competition wins twenty g's. I might have to give that nigga some."

"You so nasty. I'm not really feeling going to the Sugar Shack. You know what happened last time we went," said Yolonda. She tried making up any excuse not to have to be around Jo-Jo. Deep down she knew she still had feelings for him.

"And? Niggas is killing everywhere. You know how High Point is," said Sugar. "Shit. We got free tickets, and big ass's. Like Remy say 'The bouncers don't check us. We walk right past the metal detectors. '"

Yolonda burst out laughing at her girl. "I guess we going," she said well convinced.

***

The trio made sure that they were drop dead gorgeous. Cherry wore a black Louis Vuitton cat suit with three inch heels, her weave was pressed to the tee. Sugar wore a short Prada mini dress that catered to her long beautiful legs. Sugar was what most men called a amazon. No wonder why men were always asking her out, thought Yolonda as she applied a little Mac lip gloss to her lips. Yolonda wore a dress by Gucci that hugged her hips in all the right places. She sure picked the right dress. She checked herself out in the mirror. Cherry had did her hair in this nice crop cut sort of style that made her look immaculate.

"Bring your ass," Sugar snapped. "You always taking your precious time."

"Alright, alright." Yolonda grabbed her purse and they broke out.

"Sugar pulled up to the club in her brand new Lexus 460, parked and they got in the long line. After showing their tickets, they were escorted into the club by security. There was definitely some big time ballers inside the Sugar Shack on this particular night. They hit up the bar and got some drinks.

"Don't look now but here comes your ex." Sugar said looking in the direction of Jo-Jo.

"What up, boo." Said Jo-Jo as he kissed Yolonda on her cheek like he use to when they were together. Sad, but it took him two years and a few fucked up relationships to realize how much he took Yolanda's love for granted. He just wanted her back so things could go back like the way they use to be. "Ma, you look drop dead gorgeous. Y'all come with me." He grabbed Yolonda by the hand and lead them to V.I.P. Once there he ordered everyone shots of Patron. His plans was to fuck Yolonda tonight, maybe if he was lucky he could get her to bring Sugar Sweet and have a threesome, maybe if he was extremely lucky he could convince them to bring Cherry along and have a foursome, you know, do the damn thing!

The night was a night to remember for Yolanda. Jo-Jo kept talking her head off about how much he wanted to get his fuck on. As the night progressed, and the more shots of Patron she downed, the more gullible she was becoming.

Cherry wasn't with hanging out with Jo-Jo and his whack entourage. She wanted to be in the mix of things. She looked around and there wasn't one so called gangster in the room. This wasn't her type of party. She got up from her chair and excused herself.

Irving Projects. Q-infinity nigggas do they thing." Cherry watched a fine chocolate specimen that resembled the rap artist Camron rolling dice with like thirty niggas around him. She thought to herself, "So this is where the ballers lurking," She snuck past a huge bouncer and got a better glimpse at what was transpiring.

"Yo, yo, my roll. Seven. Um." Crook missed with eight. As the crowd got quiet, and started betting against him, he gave a slight grin. He had been stacking the dice all night long and these stupid ass niggas were too drunk to know it. He had to miss once to make fools into believers. "I raise you a grand, big timer.." Crook challenged his opponent.

"I got another grand on his next roll." Cherry blurted out as everyone looked at her like she was crazy.

"No ho's allowed. Who let this bitch in." The distraction was just the thing Crook needed to stack the dice., "Yo, Bruno. I thought you was supposed to be watching the door? Never mind. Bring mommie over here and get her a drink on me. Let's get this paper mommie." He twirled the dice in his hand and rolled sevens.

"Never doubt me," Crook said as he bent down to scoop his earnings. He glimpsed up and saw nothing but perky thighs in his face. "So, ma. What's your name is?" Damn shorty kind of reminded him of the actress Taraji P. Henson, thought Crook as he roused from his feet.

She pulled the cherry from her drink and ate it seductively. Commented, "Cherry, and yours?"

"Crook. You was my lucky charm. How you know to place your bet on me?"

She smiled. "I know a winner when I see one."

"Let me introduce you to some of the crew. That's my man Peace," he pointed. "Gun's, and Assassin. He about to go rap. Let's go check him out," said Crook. After introducing Cherry to the crew, they went out on the dance floor to watch the competition.

"Aight, aight. Second round. We only got two finalists, so come hard or don't come at all. I got Assassin from Irving Projects, and Dream from G-Boro. Shake hands and come out swinging. It's on you Dream. " The host gave Dream the mic and backed away.

"Dream get cash/ I got too much coke/ Far from being like you cause your ass is broke/ Don't fuck with me if you wise/ You should respect me like I'm God/ I know you wanna hide/ I know you wanna run/ I see it in your eyes/ You ain't flipping them pies? You keep kicking them lies/ What they call you Assassin/ Cause even in your dreams you gone hear me blasting/ And it's like that, G-Boro! Throw it up."

Assassin gritted at his opponent, and grabbed the mic out of his hand.

"They call you Dream cause you sleeping and didn't see me creeping/ Smacked you so hard you'll think you phone still ringing/ I don't know who the fuck sold you a dream? Cause if you seen the cars/ Try to get with the team/ Send you a bullet through a infrared beam/ Ask Peace? Piss a nigga off I'ma Mother-Fucking beast/ Send you back to the Boro do your boss a favor/ Assassin a hell raiser/ You sweeter than Life Savors/ And? You in a situation where the Lord can't even save ya? No disrespect. Irving Projects."

Assassin smiled cause he knew Dream's nursery rhymes wasn't hitting on shit.

As the crowd roared for Assassin, Jo-Jo's face turned sour red. Dream was one of his latest talents he had discovered out of Greensboro. He had been telling Dream to get into the studio and tighten up his rhymes. Dream acted like he was a superstar who was too good to practice, and because that, Dream had lost him a lot of money and time. Oh well, he pondered, might as well fuck Yolonda while he was in town. "Yo, waiter! Get us another drink," he motioned to get the attention of the waiter.

Sugar looked around for Cherry after realizing she was gone. That girl just couldn't sit her butt still. Sugar left the V.I.P. in search of Cherry. She looked all over, and where did she find her? In a crowded room filled with a bunch of niggas. Sugar knew Cherry was tipsy and she was worried about her, so she burst up into the room. She was quickly snatched up by a big guy with arms the size of the car tires.

"No, Bruno! That's my girl Sugar." Cherry ran to her girls aid.

"Oh, my bad, Cherry. I didn't know she was with you." Bruno sat Cherry's friend back on solid ground.

"It's ok Bruno. You don't have to apologize. You just doing your job. I be wanting to snatch her up myself sometimes too," Cherry chuckled as she sipped on her Patron. "Come on girl." Cherry lead Sugar over to where Crook and his crew was. "Sugar this Crook, and this is Gun's."

Sugar smiled and said hello. Her first impression of Gun's was, "Damn this nigga is ugly." He had the body of

50cent, jewelry like Puff and a face like Seal. he had the face only a mother could love, Sugar declared.

"We have the main event that everyone has been waiting for. We have my man Assassin, from High Point, who's been chewing them up and spitting them out. Then I have Flesh from Winston Salem, representing the Tre Four. He's been blowing everyone, he's gone against to pieces. Let's get it started. You lead off, Flesh," the host told Flesh.

Assasin swayed from side to side as his opponent kicked his rhyme.

"I'm in the game/ Hell I hustle through the pain/ I hustle in the humpty when it rain/ Shot up in the head hit my flesh/ Missed my brain/ I thank God for that/ Took my life for granted now it's raining stacks/ Assassin ain 't shit he just hold my pack/ and pray I don 't hit'em like my name the Mack/ That nigga Flesh got niggas in a choke hold/ Running home with a broke nose/ Close hisself in and check the peephole/ You know Flesh/ Change your name to ass and make you put on a dress/ You sex."

The crowd was in a uproar. They really thought Flesh was going to win. Everyone except Peace and the Q-Infinity niggas. Peace knew without a doubt that Assassin was about
to chew this nigga up and spit him out. The stakes were 2/1.

"I got twenty stacks on Assassin," Said Peace placing his bets amongst the others.

"Assassin rims/ Classic Timbs/ Bitch' s be like who the fuck is them/ Step out the car in Guess/ Looking for Flesh/ The nigga who shot you the first time/ cut him a check/ I don't really wanna beef no more/ So when I hit/ Hit him with the chrome 44/ And asked his bitch how much the ass went for/ Ain't another nigga like me/ Fuck your girl and wash my dick in the sink/ And then I go and buy a forty from them god-damn chinks/ Hold up/ Let me kick it for real." He paused and then started back rhyming. I'll make this nigga hate hisself/ Q-Infinity/ Sometimes I don't know what got into me/ Catch me on the block where the thugs and the gangsters be/ You don't wanna see a Gee/ You ain't gonna make it/ They gonna remember me."

He dropped the mic and the crowd went wild. He literally murdered Flesh.

That was the easiest twenty grand Peace ever made in his life. Peace sent Assasin a bottle of Dom Perigone to celebrate his win .

Sugar immediately left Gun 's where he was standing, and went over to Crook and Cherry. She tapped Crook on his arm.

"Yo, What up." Crook asked shorty.

"Hook me up with your friend." She nodded to the winner of the competition .

Crook looked to see who she was talking about, then yelled across the room. "Yo, Assassin. Come over here for a second." He motioned Assassin over. "Yo, this Cherry's girl, Sugar. We about to go to my place and kick it. You down?"

"It is what it is," replied Assassin. Not only was Sugar

a dime, but she resembled the R.&B singer Kelly Rowlands, he thought.

"Good. We about to bounce then," Crook said. "Yall ready, ma?" He asked Cherry.

"Give me a second. I have to to go tell my girlfriend we about to leave. I'll be right back." Sugar said.

"Hurry up." Said Crook.

Sugar damn near broke her neck to get up the steps to V.I.P. She couldn t wait to get the twenty stacks Assassin had just won from the competition.

Things were just starting to heat up between Jo-Jo and Yolonda when Sugar came flying in. Yolonda broke the kiss
and smoothed out her dress, and tried to act like Jo-Jo didn't just have his tongue down her throat.

“Yo-Yo. Me and Cherry met some cute niggas and we about to roll out. You coming or staying? If you want I can leave you the keys to my car," Said Sugar.

"I can take her home," Jo-Jo butted in, wrapping his arm around Yolonda. "We about to leave anyway."

"Cool." Sugar rolled her eyes. She didn't like Jo-Jo one bit, and hoped Yolonda wouldn't come out of her panties for his bum ass. "See yall." Sugar waved and then went and met back up with Cherry, Crook, and Assassin.

Yolonda and Jo-Jo made their way out of V.I.P. Jo-Jo had his arm around her waist and everything seemed cool, until she saw Peace and what looked like some powerful business men talking. She quickly knocked Jo-Jo's hand from around her and gave herself a little distance from him. The minute Peace noticed her, he excused himself and headed her way. He was looking so damn good! He was wearing black dress shoes and an Armani suit. She gave Peace all of her attention as he approached.

"Peace. What are you doing here?" she blushed.

"Part owner. You look nice." He took a good look at her.

"You too. I mean, you really pulled the casual thing off." She smiled admiring his attire, when Jo-Jo wrapped his arm around her waist and placed a kiss to her cheek.

"Can you please go wait for me in the car,' she frowned and shoved him away.

"Yeah, I'm at the door. Hurry up," said Jo-Jo. Ice grilling Peace.

"Yo, who is dude? When I asked you did you have a man, you specifically told me no. Now you got niggas kissing you in front of me," Peace barked.

"That's just Jo-Jo. He's in town for the weekend, and my girls left with some niggas, so he was giving me a ride home. Why you angry?" asked Yolonda.

"Cause. I was under the impression that dude hurt you. I guess I was wrong. I'm out." Peace turned out. Seeing Yolonda with another man had him 38 hot.

"Where you think you going? Listen to me when I talk to you." She grabbed his hand and made him face her. "He just taking me home. Nothing more nothing less," she said. "I promise. "

"You ain't my girl so you ain't got to explain shit. You just like every other girl I ever fucked with. "

"Fuck you, nigga. I don't have to explain shit to you. And

I would never do you like your other bitch's. I don't do the abortions, nigga," spat Yolonda. She paused once she realized everyone staring at them, and that she was way out of pocket. "I'm sorry, Peace," she said as he walked off. Damn. She went and found Jo-Jo, who wasn't too far being that he had been watching the whole ordeal. She got into Jo-Jo's 7 Series Beamer and sat in silence. The whole ride to her house, he kept trying to say the words to get her to fuck him.

"I really missed you. I think we should be a couple again," said Jo-Jo.

"Take me home, nigga. And stop touching me. " She removed his hand from her thigh. "What happened to your other bitch's? Did you finally find out that they were after your money?" She couldn't wait until Jo-Jo pulled up to her apartment complex. She opened the door and got out the car without saying a word. She went in her apartment and cried her heart out for saying what she said to Peace. She was wrong and he didn't deserve all of what she had said.

***

Crook, Cherry, Sugar and Assassin chilled at Crooks bedroom flat smoking purple haze. Cherry looked at Crook. She was ready to see if his fine ass had a nice size gat. She got up out of her chair and walked over to Crook and whispered in his ear.

"I want you, big boy."

With no questions asked, Crook lead Cherry to his bedroom. He took off his shirt and began to kiss Cherry passionately. He made his way to the cherry tattoo on her neck. Seemed like every kiss drove her crazy!

Cherry came out of her outfit, and sat on the foot of the bed, and pulled him onto her. Crook sucked on her neck trying to leave passion marks, "This your spot," He wanted to know.

"No. Not really, boo. You're getting close. See if you can find it." She arched her back as he went down to her aroused nipples and traced his tongue around her areola's. The way Crook sucked her breast had her going insane. She couldn't wait until he was deep inside of her.

Crook crept down to her belly button and noticed her body start to flutter. That was the response he needed. He went down to her triangle shaped vagina and planted his tongue in the middle of her patch. He ate the pussy like grapes. After he got her soaking wet, and she climaxed, he wiped his face, sat up, took off his pants, and reached in his pocket for protection.

"Let me help you with that," Cherry insisted as she reached for the condom, opened it, strapped it onto him, and then straddled him. She gyrated her hips and rocked back and forth as they got lost into each other.

"You gonna talk to your little girlfriend all night on the phone and act like I'm not here?" Sugar asked Assassin. He had been talking to his little girlfriend for more than an hour and her patience was wearing thin. She should've robbed this nigga by now, fucked him to sleep, stole the money he had won, and then grabbed up Cherry so they could get the fuck out of dodge.

"I'ma get at you, Peaches." Assassin hung up his cell and sat down beside Sugar. He placed his arm around her shoulder. "What up with the shade,"

"Cause, I came over here to chill with you and you haven't even looked at me. I'm not your type or something?"

"Sorry bout that, you're very attractive. At first, Iwas like, shorty a groupie, gold digger, or probably didn't want to fuck with a nigga my age," He kicked his Timb boots on the table while smoking on purple haze.

She was really offended by what Assassin said. "So, exactly how old are you anyway?" she inquired waiting for his reply.

"Seventeen in a half,"

"What. You a little boy? I thought you were older. Boy, I can't fuck with you. I know you're not ready for me." She replied as she gave a slight chuckle, embarrassed that she was fucking with a young ass tenderoni. He was jail bait!

Assassin got up and went to the next room leaving sugar by herself. Bitch's always got to tripping once they found out his age.

Sugar laughed out laugh, "seventeen. He's cute and all, but he is too damn young. I'm almost four years older than him. Damn. I'ma have to buy his young ass a game boy, she reasoned to herself.

Assassin laid on the bed talking to Peaches as Sugar came in the door. He watched Sugar take off her dress and get in the bed with him. He was speechless.

Sugar grabbed the phone up out of his hand.. "He's busy right now!" she said to his girlfriend, she could hear the operator as she ended his call.

Assassin came out of his shirt, and took her exposed breast in his mouth.

"Ahh shit that hurts." She remarked as she rubbed his baby face, "I ain't going nowhere." She moaned as he took his time giving her C Cup breast the attention they needed.

She stopped bitching and complaining when Assassin went down below. Do your thing. Young nigga! She thought as he licked her inner thighs in a circular motion, causing her body to tremble. She begged him not to stop. "Oh, gosh!" She called out as she stirred his face between her legs. "Stop teasing me." She cried out. "Come on." She guided him up. She needed to feel him deep inside her. She guided his thick long dick inside of her warm gushy pussy and started gyrating her hips back and forth and side to side. Assassin went hard in the paint. She thought as she bit down upon her bottom lip as he dashed in and out of her with deep long strokes. He had her long legs stretched out like it was nobody s business.

She maneuvered herself from the missionary style into the reverse cowgirl and rode him backwards. "Tell me you love this pussy."Demanded Sugar.

"Yeah, I love it, I'm about to cum," before she could budge he popped off.

"Shit! You forgot to put on a condom," She mentioned as semen dripped down her thighs.

Shit. Assassin could give two shits about going raw dawg. He kept right on stroking Sugar's fine ass. When she tried to get up to clean off, he pulled her back down on his rock hard erection and went for seconds.

The next morning, Sugar woke up with a sore everything. Assassin had ripped her up. She had to give it up. He was a good sexing motherfucker! She glimpsed at his pants on the floor, filled with nothing but hundred dollar bills. She was about to take his money until she remembered how he had made love to her last night. No one had ever fucked her twice in one outing, and ate her pussy the way he had, she decided to give him a pass this time because a nigga like him only came once every blue moon.

CHAPTER 6

Maybe nobody loves me? Maybe that's the reason I'm single. I wonder if Peace loves me, pondered Yolonda as she shopped at the mall. She purchased a lot of expensive clothes, but the clothes wasn't for her. She left the mall and drove to Irving Projects. She hated Irving Projects because they were some of the most dangerous projects in High Point, NC. You had Daniel Brooks, Clara Cox, J.C Morgan, Springfield, Farmington, Juanita Hills, Springfield, Spring Valley, New Gate, Carson Stout, But to her Irving Projects were the most grimiest of them all. She hoped she didn't have to kill one of these fools. Thought Yolonda as she activated the alarm to her Benz and got out of the car. She noticed a crowd full of guys huddled around at a dice game.

"Do you all know where I can find Peace?" she questioned while holding onto the gift bags she had tightly.

"Who's looking for him." Inquired a guy with a serious scar on his face.

"Yolonda. I have some clothes I think he might want."

"Shorty," The guy with the scar across his face said. "Go take her to see Peace." he then went back to rolling dice.

Yolonda followed Shorty through the flight of stairs. Other than her passing by Irving Projects she had never been in them before. Broken bottles, syringes, crack vials, and a reeking odor that she would never forget. She stepped over a dope fiend as they nodded off on the staircase. Little kids bounced around gracefully, smacking the dope fiends that were nodding off.

"How come we didn't just use the elevator?" she asked.

"Broken," replied Shorty.

She should have guessed.

"We're almost there," Shorty said climbing the many steps to get to Peace's floor.

"Good, thought Yolonda. Her feet were killing her. If she was correct, then they were on the 10th floor. Lawd she hoped she didn't run into Peace's girlfriend Trish.

Yolonda pulled out a twenty dollar bill from out of her purse to give to Shorty.

"Nah, keep it, ma. Any friend of Peace's is a friend of mine," He gave her a kindly smirk, tapped on the door and walked away.

Damn Peace had a lot of respect around this bitch, she came to the conclusion as she waited at the door.

Peace opened the door wide open and was shocked to see that it was Yolonda. "What are you doing here,"

She stepped into the apartment and glimpsed around at all the drugs money and guns on the table, and answered. "looking for you, bae. I stopped by the mall and I saw some things I wanted to get you. I hope you like them," she handed him the bags. "If not I can always take them back and replace them."

Peace checked the sizes of the clothing and everything was good. "How you know my size,"

She smiled for the first time. "Because you my man, Zaddy!" She kissed him on his kissable lips and rubbed his cute face and enchanting beard as she gazed into his eyes, while she was doing so she noticed the giggles of laughter that flooded the room, she also noticed Peace's demeanor changed as his crew teased him.

"Source money," Guns commented.

""Mr? Lover man," Crook chuckled.

"What are you making that face for," Yolonda crossed her arms over her breast region and glared at Peace.

"Didn't I tell you about that fly ass mouth? Now go take my shit to your car and go wait for me," he snapped, putting on a scene for his niggas.

Was he serious? Thought Yolanda. He might've had his niggas fooled but not her, she let her man be a man. She swallowed her pride. "Okay, hurry up Peace. I'll be in the car," She let out a frustrating sigh. As she was walking off she could hear someone singing. Peace and Yolanda sitting in the tree K.I.S.S.I.N.G. She laughed as Peace closed the door behind her.

"Yo, Assassin. How she look man? Think I should make her my down ass chick.

Assassin answered back, "You'll be a fool not to. Shorty like that!"

"Shorty tight! Hook me up with one of her girls," Guns butted in.

"I got you." Peace lied. Guns ugly ass was always wanting someone to hook him up. Peace headed to meet up With Yolanda. He was treated like a star in the hood. Little kids, hustlers, and wanna be hustlers paid him homage as he made his way onto the courtyard. He was the only person who gave a fuck when it came to the hood. He was the one paid for the Girls and Boys club across the street and every weekend from 7:30 a.m to 10:00 a.m he made sure that every single kid and crack head had a decent meal, it was his way of giving back to the community. Upon reaching Yolonda s vehicle, the ice cream truck bent the corner. The kids that were getting wet by the fire hydrant, and the kids lurking ran up to Peace. This was an everyday ritual.

"You want ice cream?" Peace asked Yolanda while the kids crowded up around him to get ice cream.

"Yeah, grab me a strawberry crunch," She told him. Peace was so generous she thought as she sat in the car and watched Peace purchase every kid the ice cream of their choice. Not one of the fifty kids or more went without. She wanted to get to know the real Peace, what he was really about. She was straight up crushing on him.

She patted her leg as she listened to Jill Scott's "Is it the way," trying not to let Peace know how attracted she thought he was as he got into the car.

Peace noticed that Yolonda kept her eyes glued on him.

"Where too, we headed to your place?" she asked him.

"You driving. That shit you pulled at the club had me heated. I started to kick your narrow ass. Is that why you got me the clothes and shit?" he asked as he went through the gift bags.

"Sorry. I did feel bad. That night I actually cried myself to sleep wishing I hadn't of said that to you. You didn't deserve that and I was wrong. I was just upset that you didn't trust me." She watched Peace look off into space. She placed her hand on his thigh while eating ice cream. "If you want to know. I cursed Jo-Jo out, bae,"

"What up with all this bae shit. You gotta be real to be with me. I'm not looking for love right now," he said as she pulled into the parking deck.

"I'm real. Everything about me is. You should give props where they're due. You have a girl with more money than you, with more determination than you, and brings more to the table than you," remarked Yolonda.

"You got life fucked up, shorty. You should be happy to be around a nigga like me. I don't brag about money cause I don't have too. But trust when I tell you. You don't come close. Can believe this chick," he mumbled under his breath.

"Yeah. Whatever, nigga. You still a block hustler. As long as you have me you good thou." she laughed. She loved pissing Peace off.

"Boom! Peace slammed the car door behind him and went into the house. Yolonda was getting on his last nerve.

Yolonda debated whether or not to follow Peace, or just leave. He was a straight hater. It wasn't her fault that her hand called for doe. She took the elevator to Peace's studio flat. He had left the door ajar for her, so she let herself in and took a seat on the couch as Peace's dog Gambino growled at her. He was just like Peace. Always acting hard.

She grabbed the remote and flipped to the channel 8 news. As usual there was a lot of killing going on in the city. When would these niggas stop wilding, is what she asked herself.

Peace hit the dial on his radio and listened to his Capone & Noreago's blood money Cd. He then went to his weight bench and started to workout.

Yolonda tried to watch the news but couldn't, instead she watched Peace as he lifted two hundred and twenty five pounds for sets of ten, Damn he was chiseled. She wasn't too interested in the chaos that was going on in the city any longer, she fixed her eyes upon Peace until he got up and went to the bathroom. She could hear water running. She sat and wondered if she should join him in the shower or not. As she wondered loud banging at the door took her out of her lustful thinking.

"Open the door, nigga. It's Just. I got Goldshay with me,"

"Goldshay." She got up from the sofa and said to herself. She went into the bathroom. She could see Peace's silhouette behind the glass. She opened the shower door.

Peace almost had a heart attack. "What the fuck is your problem busting up in here like that?"

"Someone named Just at the door. He said he got some bitch named Goldshay with him.

Who is she?" she questioned with crossed arms. "Are you fucking her," she asked glancing down at his huge swipe.

"Get the door for me and tell Just to have a seat. Throw me a towel." he wiped the soap from his eyes.

"Yolonda grabbed the towel and tossed it on the floor. She pissed the hell off and ready to show her ass. She went and snatched the door open. "He said to have a seat. Don't touch shit, and be quiet while I watch tv." Yolonda sat back on the sofa agitated that Peace's boy had brung some bitch's over.

Justice, Bree, and Goldshay took a seat on the sofa as Peace's chick rolled her eyes at them. Peace never told Justice about shorty. He knew about Trish, but hell, Trish didn't even know about the studio flat. He had to be nosy.

"What's your name."

{What) "What you want to know my name for? I don't know you, I don't wanna know you, and I m trying to watch tv,"

"Yo, Just. I see you met Yolanda. She has a fly ass mouth as you can see. What I tell you about that mouth, ma." Peace remarked in his wife beater and basketball shorts.

Yolanda rolled her eyes at Peace and continued to watch tv.

"Son, we were about to go out to Becky's and wanted to see if you wanted to roll with us, but I see you and your girl bonding and everything," stated Just.

"Then why don't you leave," Yolanda's response.

"Woe!" Just placed his hands up in retreat.

"Come on, Yolanda. Becky's got some bomb ass chicken" Peace tried convincing her.

"Is you out of your mind? I just got here. Don't you see I'm deep into this, she flipped the tv on something better to watch, being a little extra. "I really want to see this. Watch it with me. If you're hungry I will cook something," She said. "Come watch this with me," She patted the spot beside her for him to join her on the couch.

Just watched as Peace sat down beside his new lady. This nigga was in love and shit! Thought Just. "I'ma roll a couple of blunts of Purple before I bounce. Yo, can I holler at you for a minute." He stood to his feet and waited for Peace to get up before he went into Peace's room. When Peace got into the room, he said. "Son, I like that little piece right there. But yo, You know Goldshay been asking about you. That's the reason we came over here," He laughed

Yolonda really couldn't stand to be around the two raggedy heffah's sitting in Peace's living-room, so she got up from the couch and went into the kitchen to find something to cook. She opened the refrigerator and found slice turkey and cheese.

In less then ten minutes she had fried them two sandwiches a piece. Not bad considering he had no real food in his fridge. She grabbed a pack of Lays Potato chips from out of the counter, then grabbed two twenty ounce Sprite's from out the fridge. She juggled everything to the living-room table in the front of the T.V. so her and Peace could kick it and chill. She watched as the two girls Peace's partner Just brung over as they started to laugh and giggle. They were probably jealous. Yolonda didn t like them and she was about to let them know.

"Is something funny to yall? I don't appreciate yall coming in my man s crib with that disrespect. I will whup a bitch ass up in here. Yeah, act like you want it, bitch," said Yolonda to the tall dark skinned heffa who couldn't seem to keep the sneaky grin off her face.

"What's going on now?" asked Peace as he stepped out of the room.

"These girls your friend brung over here laughing cause I cooked you turkey sandwiches. I don't like how they disrespecting you. I had to voice my opinion." Yolonda crossed her arms, cocked her neck to the side and cut her eyes at the two nappy headed heffahs.

"You right. Just. Get at me tomorrow. They can't be disrespecting the way a nigga eating," said Peace giving Just a dap of the hand.

"Yo, word. We out," replied Just as he, Bree and Goldshay made their departure.

Peace sat down on the sofa and took a bite of the sandwich. "Damn you did your thing, ma. They don't know what they missing. "

Yolonda smiled. For the first time Peace reasoned with her. After they ate, Yolonda grabbed a pillow from the sofa, fluffed it out and rested on Peace's lap as they watched Tyler Perry's "Why Did I Get Married. " She looked up at Peace. He seemed to be deep in thought. "What's wrong?" she asked.

"It's late. What time you leaving?"

"Don't worry about me leaving. Why? your boy about to double back or something with them busted looking heffah's?" she laughed.

"I told you about your mouth. " He playfully shoved her head to the side.

"So." Yolonda jumped up swinging. Peace let her give

him a couple punches to the body before scooping her up on his shoulder and carrying her to his room, where he sat her across his King sized bed. They began to kiss passionately. Yolonda had never been kissed the way he was kissing her. Ever. he was a good kisser she thought as she helped him come out of his clothes. She peeled off his shirt, then slid her hands down to his big dick. She rubbed him and was instantly aroused. "Take me, Peace. "

"You want it?" He asked.

"Yeah, Don't talk. " She placed her finger over his mouth to quiet him. Then picked up where she left off. Kissing him and then climbing onto his lap.

"This is my pussy right here?" asked Peace as he cuffed her plump ass.

"For crying out loud, yeah, it's yours. " She began to trace kisses along his neck. Damn she wanted him.

"Do you want me?" he held her back so they could talk for a minute.

"Yeah. I want you. Bad! Now can you please stop cutting me off?" She was starting to get agitated. She shoved him back onto the bed and began kissing him aggressively.

Peace restrained Yolonda. "Hold up. I like you too." He grabbed her hands and sat up. "But I'm not with waking up knowing you won't be here. I think we should get to know each other before we fuck. I hope you understand?"

The weakest shit she had ever heard. "Peace. Don't do this. If you like me then you'll just go with the flow. Is it Trish," she wanted to know.

"Don't worry about Trish. Trust me. Let's get some

sleep. I'm tired." He wrapped his arm around her and held her tight.

Yolonda wanted to give Peace a few choice words, but to tell the truth she did like being in his warm embrace. Before she knew what happened someone was shaking her awake.

"Get up. I need you to drop me off at the spot. I gotta make moves so I can be as big as you are one day." he taunted her.

"Give me a minute," She rolled over and tossed the blanket over her head. "Stop being an asshole." She said as Peace continued to shake her awake.

"Peace snatched the covers off the bed. "Get up. The early birds get the worms."

"Fuck that." She got up and stretched out.

"Ma. You grumpy in the a.m. Get that drool off your face. The toothbrush in the cabinet in the bathroom.

Yolonda got up, brushed her teeth and got herself together. Afterwards she took Peace to his hustle grounds. "Bye." She said as she pulled in front of Irving Projects.

"You ain't gonna leave like that. Give your boy some sugar." He leaned over and kissed Yolonda.

"Is it too late to go back to your place?" she asked in the middle of their kiss.

"If you care about me like you say , and it's not all about the sex thing then call me and let me know that you thinking about me." Peace handed her a piece of paper with his name and number written on it then emerged from the car.

Yolonda looked at the number and pulled off.

***

"What I wouldn't do to get a piece of that. Mommie. Come over her and holler at your boy. I won t bite."

"What's your name sexy," Yolonda asked the lusting driver of a shiny Seven series red Beamer.

"Whatever you want it to be." He flossed his platinum jewelry in shorty's face as his crew looked on.

"Are those diamonds real, or are you perpetrating?" asked Yolonda. She had been around the South Side area for weeks plotting on Cash and his crew. She knew enough to know that he was the boss and supplied most of the city with coke, pills, weed, and heroin.

"Everything about me is real. Where are you headed to gorgeous." Asked Cash. There was no way on God's green earth that he was letting this sexy ass girl pass through without shooting his shot.

"I have some business to take care of," she replied as she walked off in her tight denim blue Daisy Dukes, white Christian Dior top with matching pumps.

"Hold up, Short. Here. Take my number." Cash went in his car and got a pen from his glove compartment and wrote down his name and number. "What's your name." He asked her.

She stopped walking. "Jasmine."

"Check it. Jasmine." He smiled. "Take my number and give me a call."

She could tell that he was trying to impress his crew. She took the number out of his hand.

Stated. " Maybe I will call," and walked off. It was easy to entice men in a tight pair of coochie cutters. She couldn't wait to find out where Cash was keeping all of his dope so she and her girls could move in on him.

CHAPTER 7

Peace, Assassin, Guns, and Crook smoked on hydro as they chilled at one of their many trap spots waiting for Just to come back with the work. They were out of work and the fiends were still juking, coming back every five minutes to see if they had got straight yet.

"Damn, where was Just at?" Thought Peace. He picked up his cell, but before he could place the call his shit rung. He checked the screen and noticed Just's number. "Yo, where the fuck are you?" asked Peace.

"Out front. Yo. Narcs everywhere. Clean that shit up and get the fuck out the house." Justice looked around at what looked like the police convention. He backed his Suburban up and bust a u-turn.

Peace gave Assassin all the guns, scale and told him to break out. After he left. He then wiped everything down.

The clique was just about to bounce when they were interrupted.

"Boom!" It was the High Point Police kicking down the door and making their way in. "Get on the ground! ."

Everyone remained cool. It was definitely some foul play, thought Peace as he and the crew laid on the floor face first.

"Well, well, well. If it isn't Peace Vanchez? I hear you doing big things around here. Thought by switching up your spot that you could throw us off, huh? Where's the shit at? As long as you have enemies we'll keep running up in your shit. Better watch the company you keep. I plan to have you and the rest of your Q-Infinity clique doing NBA numbers before the basketball season even gets started. Pat these bitch 's down and turn this unfurnished drug house upside down," lead Narcotic Wolf shouted.

After hours of harassments and threats, Officer Wolf became a ticking time bomb. His reliable source was close but not accurate. Officer Wolf knew he wouldn't be getting any rest until he took these hoodlums down. And besides that, he knew if he was able to bring down Peace and his notorious Q-Infinity gang then that would make his ranking go up. Probably Detective, nah, probably more like Chief of Police. He thought big. He had to catch Peace and his little foot soldiers with something, even if he had to go against his oath which he swore upon. Now if he could only find a rat out the crew, or someone to make a couple big controlled buys. It wouldn't be long before Peace slipped up. There was no need to hold them any longer. Officer Wolf walked up to Peace and lifted him up off the ground. He looked at him with eyes filled with hatred. "Mr. Vanchez. You ass-holes can get back to your destruction. Un-cuff them," he said to his fellow officers. "But I'm warning you that I'm onto you. It's only gonna be a matter of time," he stated. "Every time you see a cop you better pray to God it's not me. Ha, ha, ha." Wolf laughed as he and his twenty man crew left.

"Damn. Fuck Wolf. He can suck my dick," Peace said brushing the dust off his shirt. "Nobody ain't stopping me from getting this money, " he stated.

"You think we should switch spots?" Crook asked.

"One thing's for sure. We got twenty-four hours before they can get another search warrant," Replied Peace.

That night Peace and his gang hustled around the clock. Seemed like they made more money in one night then they did the whole week after the police left. As the sun started to come up, Peace looked at his Movado watch that read 7.30 a.m. He called up Just. Just answered with the sleepy voice.

"Yo," Just said as he glanced at the naked girl beside him whose name he couldn't remember.

"I need you to bring me three biscuits cause I'm hungry." Peace spoke in codes. Three biscuits were the equivalence of three kilos.

"Word. Be there in a few." Just let him know. He tapped shorty and woke her up. Minutes later he was shoving her into a taxi. He got into his Suburban and took the three biscuits to Peace. He pulled up to the complex Peace was in and saw the new lookouts Peace had hired. Good he thought as got out of his vehicle and checked out the scene. "What up, Trigger, Scoop," He nodded towards the young watch-outs.

"What up, Just." Scoop nodded as he called Peace up on the walkie talkie.

Just went up to the tenth floor where Peace and them were trapping at. Big Killer was posted up in front of the door with an AK-47. Peace wasn't playing any games. Just reasoned as he walked past Killer's heavy frame. What a big ugly son-of-a-bitch. Just said to himself. He gave Peace the book bag with the work in it and took a seat on the sofa.

Peace gave Assassin, Crook, and Guns their own bird. "You fellas think y'all can handle a bird?"

"Yeah," Everyone nodded in unison.

"Crook,. I want you over at Brenda's apartment on the six floor. Guns. I want you on the 12th floor at Jay's spot. and you go to Ms. Jones house," Peace said to Assassin.

"Hold up. Why that little nigga get to start off where all the money coming to? " Gun's wanted to know. "Maybe you should let me handle this floor. I've been in real combat before," said Gun's. "And besides, he's just a kid." Gun's was annoyed about the fact that Peace put Assassin in a better position than him.

Just shook his head from side to side. This nigga Gun's is gonna be a problem. He thought.

"Don't question what I do. We a team so act like it," stated Peace before rolling out with Just.

***

Assassin knew he was supposed to be at the spot, but it had been a few days since he last talked to Sugar. He knocked on the door to her apartment and was greeted by his down ass chick.

Damn. Sugar thought to herself. She forgot she had

given Assassin her address. She smiled surprised as she wrapped her arms around his tall frame. Assassin was a little taller than her. Around 6,2, 190 with light brown skin, he reminded her of the rap artist Memphis Bleek.

"What brings you around my way?" She asked with her hand propped against the door frame.

"You." He answered as he went up under her arm and made his way to the sofa and propped his Timb boots on her glass living room table.

"Ashtray?" He inquired.

"Get your boots off my table. Do you know how much that table cost me." She went bonkers. She huffed and then grabbed an ashtray from off the entertainment system and gave it to him.

"Calm down. You miss your boy." He asked. "I had a rough day and I wasn't trying to argue. I just came to see my main squeeze. Come here, mommie."

"She smiled from ear to ear. Assassin had a hell'ava swagger. And the boy could dress like a young Puff Daddy. She thought as she began to kiss his kissable lips. "You know I missed you." She replied, helping him to get out of his shirt and unbuckled his belt until the doorbell rang.

Sugar stopped what she was doing and went to go see who was at the door. She checked the peek-hole and saw that it was Yolonda. Shit! she thought to herself. This couldn't be happening. "put your shirt back on," she said to Assassin. "Hurry up."

"Open up. I know you in there girl," said Yolonda ringing the doorbell like she was crazy.

"Fuck that." Assassin said smoking his blunt and

gripping his 9mm in case some shit popped off.

"Please!" She begged. Seeing that he was gonna show his ass she unlatched the door. "What up, Yo-Yo?" she asked embarrassed. Afraid that Yolonda's nosy ass would find out that Assassin was jail bate.

"Don't what's up me. Somebody getting they freak on up in here," said Yolonda busting into Sugar' s apartment. "You Peace's homeboy?" she asked. "You and Sugar fucking."

Sugar wanted to run and hide. She just hoped to God Yolonda didn't ask his age.

"You gotta ask her," Assassin said as he groped his dick and looked at Sugar.

Yolonda looked at Sugar and then back at him after Sugar didn't reply. "Where is Peace? I haven't heard from him in
a couple of days. I keep getting his voice mail," said Yolonda.

"Shit kinda hot so he been laying low. So, you the chick that came by the spot the other day ," asked Assassin.

"Yep. Chick named Yolonda. Can I hit that blunt?" he passed the blunt to her and she asked, "What's your name?"

"Assassin." He laughed as she started to choke on the hydro.

"Girl. What's wrong with you?" Yolonda asked Sugar. You with Assassin so now you ain't got time for your girl? I'm out. Tell Peace I said to call me." She gave Assassin back
his blunt. "Bye bitch," she said to Sugar as she left out the door.

"Bye ho. Don't come back. " Sugar yelled as she closed the door and locked it. "Now where were we. " She smiled and walked over to Assassin. They began to kiss passionately. Assassin tried to pick her up but she applied her weight down. "You know you can't pick me up.

Assassin picked her up with ease and carried her to her room. He laid her down on the bed and pulled down her leggin tights. He began to kiss her Victoria Secret Peach bikini laced panties. She was so damp he thought as he continued to scan his tongue across her slit while lifting up her shirt at the same time. He gripped her round breast as she slid her panties to the side and began to suck her moist pussy lips. "You like that?" he asked.

"Yeah, baby," she said as her head tilted back and he licked her all around. "It feels really good." She cringed.

Assassin went in and out of Sugar with his tongue as she gyrated her hips from side to side. He laid on his back as Sugar sat on his face. He had her moaning until his face was filled with her juices. Sugar helped Assassin out of his jeans. She pulled him to her and he spent her around in the doggy style position. She rolled with the punches as he dashed in and out of her with his fat cucumber sized dick. Assassin was a freak in the sheets and could do it well. She swayed her hips as he fucked the shit out of her. She knew she should've made him wear a condom, but he was just too big for any condom, and so damn innocent, she thought as he pulled out of her and then crammed his way back inside.

"I'm coming, baby," she cried out as Assassin plowed in and out of her. She was so happy when he finally climaxed and flopped down beside her on the bed. Damn he had fucked the dog shit out of her. She watched him get up and start to put on his clothes. "Where are you going?" she asked.

"To the spot." He got dressed, put on his sneakers, kissed Sugar Sweet and then bounced. As he was leaving Sugar's crib on the South Side of town, he was approached by Chip and his dick beaters. Assassin always had problems with Chip and his gang. They would always steal his rhyme books and pick fights with him. That was then and this was now. He held his hand on the gun concealed in his waist with caution and stopped walking.

"What up, Carlos?" Chip asked trying to shake Assassin's
hand.

"Why you using my government? Assasssin to you, chump. " He turned down Chip's hand and asked, "What yall want. A pack or something?"

Chip smirked. Thinking, "This conceited bastard. " He wanted to deck Assassin in his smart mouth, but instead shook off the insult. "Nah. I don't need no pack, but I would like to show everybody how garbage you are," Chip said so everyone in his neighborhood could witness the victory he was about to get.

"Oh, is that right." Assassin rubbed the few strings of hair on his chin. "Start it up," he said as everyone gathered around
to see the battle that was about to take place.

Peace rounded the corner on the South Side right in front of Taylor St. Apartments when he saw a gang of people and what looked like Assassin. What was Assassin doing all the way on the South Side, he thought as he pulled up to the scene. It was just a freestyle battle Peace realized as he looked on.

"I remember when I used to kick your ass after class/ And chase your ass home just to make you mad/ You was writing in your pad/ I threw your rhymes away/ Them old ass rhymes you probably spitting today/ Them happy ass rhymes I used to think you was gay/ Peace made you who you is today/ A fall guy so he let you stay/ Them niggas that you wit' can't save you from Chip/ I walk around wit' the whole 17 in my clip/ Now Chip, Chip, Chip/ That's the sound of my gun/ Killed Assassin now your boy is done ."

"Ohh. Ahh! " The crowd roared as Chip shitted on Assassin in the worst way.

"I can see why you stole my note pad/ Using my rhymes I guess I am that bad/ I got niggas who keep calling me out/ Toe to toe with me and you'll be crawling out/ My clique be ballen out/ Don P. sipping/ Mercedes Benz wippen/ He walking the block with all his friends wit'em/ I ain't Pac I ain't Big, but I can get you a gig/ Have you shining shoes take your girl on a cruise/ Different colored stones like I'm Indiana Jones your bitch give good brains I can't leave that thing alone/ She scream Assassin damn your shit is so long/ She flip over roll over then she strap back on/ Every time I smack that ass it turns the bitch on. Yo, Chip. Crawl up out of here before I get to spittin for real. Assassin that deal." Assassin felt good as the crowd gave him his props. He knew Chip was flaming hot. He looked up and saw Peace's SUV. He gave Chip dap and made his way to Peace's

Range Rover.

"What up?" asked Assassin with a grin on his face as he gave Peace dap.

"Same shit, just a different day," Peace said passing Assassin the blunt he had lit as he got into the passenger seat of the SUV.

"Damn you killed that nigga," said Peace. "But yo, on the real. You gotta stay off the South Side cause you know them niggas don't really fuck with us." Peace warned. Peace knew he had to do something to keep Assassin out of trouble. Assassin was too talented to be out here in these streets, and Peace knew this so he had been working on getting Assassin hot producers and studio time. "Yo, guess what?"

"What?" asked Assassin as he puffed the good dro.

"I got this kid named the Specialist to produce some hot beats for you." Peace pulled off and gave Assassin the details.

CHAPTER 8

Where was this nigga? He was such an asshole. Yolanda sat in her chair waiting for Cash. He was thirty minutes late for their dinner at Giorgio s. To make things worse she had been avoiding Peace because of Cash. She was sure if she continued to see Peace that it would make it impossible to focus on robbing Cash. Peace was the type of man that made a woman want to find a job, get herself together and raise a family. She was knocked out of her trance of thought when Cash kissed her on the cheek. Cash was cute. Dark skin complexed with the physique of a football player. He was tall about 6ft. He wasn't the best looking nigga but he was paid out the ass. If it wasn't for that she wouldn't even be wasting her time on him. She couldn't believe he was wearing True Religion and Jordan s to a five star restaurant. Talk about hood. Maybe this was going to be harder than she thought. They ordered dinner and ate. And then Cash pulled out a large sum of money and paid the bill. They walked out of Giorgio s hand and hand.

Cash begged her to take a ride with him so she left her

car at the restaurant and got into the car with him. Cash mashed the gas and took off in his Aston Martin. As he zig zagged through traffic showing off, Yolanda held on for dear life. Cash pulled up on a block filled with hustlers. He was approached by a young thug. He rolled down the driver side window. "Yo, Chip. You got that money you owe me?"

Chip went in his pocket and handed Cash a large stack of money. "You know I got that. You got me on that other thing?" Chip asked.

Cash reached up under this seat and pulled out a large bag of white substance. "You know I got you, play-boy! What's
been going on out here on the strip?" asked Cash as he checked out the scene.

"Just flowed this cat named Assassin out. I'm telling you, you need to get me some studio time. Dude nice but I'm
nicer. I left that nigga in a coma." Chip bragged. "I embarrassed that nigga. I wish you could've seen it." he exaggerated.

"Oh yeah. You better not lose to them lame ass niggas. By the way. This my girl, Jasmine?" Cash changed the subject. "Nice to meet you, Jasmine?" Chip nodded. "I don't wanna keep the customers waiting," Chip said as he stepped off.

"I gotta stop by the crib to put this money up. Roll with me. I don't wanna be riding around with all this shit on me. it will only take a minute, " Cash said.

"Cool." Yolonda replied. She could use this opportunity

to find out where Cash lived and where he kept his stash at. After hours of driving they pulled up to Cash's mansion. He was living lavishly. A gated home. A Rolls Royce, Bentley, Beamer, and a collection of high powered motor cycles. He used his code to get inside. Now this was living. Thought Yolonda. She had never met a guy with so much money. Cash parked and they went inside. She followed him upstairs and took a seat on his spacious bed as he counted the money Chip had given him. She watched him place the money in the closet. She assumed he had a safe that he kept his money in.

Cash returned and began to kiss Yolonda. They kissed until she almost went. As Cash rubbed her breast she removed his hands. "Slow down. I can't go there with you just yet. It's too early and I Don't get down like that. Please, stop. Stop Cash!" she pleaded.

Cash acted as if he couldn't hear and kept right on kissing her. "Boy, stop! Nice try." She shoved him back and sat up on the bed. Cash was getting too aggressive if you asked her. "Let's go. I need to get back to my car. Come on." She grabbed his hand and guided him out of the house and to the car. When they got to Giorgio's where she left her car, she let out a sigh. They kissed for what seemed like an eternity and then she broke the kiss and walked to her car.

Cash pulled up beside Jasmine as she got into the car.

"Yo, Jasmine. Just go with the flow. Whenever your ready to be the queen let me know. Remember that's your castle," he added before pulling off.

Yolonda smiled as she started the car and pulled off. She

was kinda digging Cash a little.

Peace, Just, Crook, and Guns drunk Hennessey as they waited for Assassin to show up at the studio.

Meanwhile, Sugar, Yolanda, and Cherry got ready for Assassin to pick them up. He was late for his first demo. Sugar wiggled into a tight Christian Dior skirt as she peered into the mirror. She wanted Assassin's eyes to be on her and her only. The sound of the horn caused her to grab her Christian Dior handbag and hurry to Assassin's Tahoe. She kissed Assassin's cheek as she and her girls got in. Assassin pulled off in a rush. His vehicle wasn't flashy. No rims, just tinted windows, Tv's and a booming sound system. In less than ten minutes, Assassin and the girls made their way into Omega studio on North Main street. A cloud of smoke was up in the air, and Assassin was surrounded by his Q-infinity family and loved ones. He rolled up a few blunts before going into the booth.

Yolanda made her way over to Peace. She hadn't saw him in God's no telling how long. But he was looking so sexy with his platinum necklace, Cartier shades, lumberjack shirt, denim jeans, and Polo boots. She glimpsed over at Cherry who was all up on some cute nigga named Crook, and then at Sugar who was ignoring some nigga named Guns. Yolanda listened to Assassin as he dropped his new demo. (Hunger).

"You niggas leave me with no choice. I want the Bentley and new Porsche/ why I can't have a Ferrari and Rolls Royce/ you hear the hunger in my voice!"

Was the sound of Assassin's new demo.

As things wound down and the specialist played the

track. Assassin asked if everyone was feeling his new demo. Everyone loved it except for Sugar.

"What's wrong, ma?" asked Assassin. "You not feeling that shit? Why you look depress?"

"Cause, you ain't let me do the hook," Sugar said catching reckless stares. "What? I can sing," was her reply.

"Girl, don't embarrass me up in here. I've heard your voice," Yolonda teased.

"Come on in the booth." He went over some details with Sugar and got the Specialist to drop the beat. Thirty minutes later they performed.

"For every woman who is willing to support their man in each and every way. I know I got my man s back," As the beat dropped Sugar Sweet began the hook.

"I'll blast for you/ get cash for you/ I'll do anything that you ask me to/ Let's get it." She smiled as Assassin came in on que.

"Mommie you know I'm wit' it but If we do get this cash then you know we gon' split it/ lay you on the bed with the money and you know I'm gon/ hit it/ Never knew that you could be so down/ Once we linked up seemed like was we running the town/ If a nigga got locked it would be you that would be holding me down/ still got doe cause you would be making them rounds,"

Sugar cut in. "I'll blast for you/ Get cash for you/ I'll do anything that you ask me to/ Let's get it."

"My girl like five eight/ Light brown with the Eryka Badu face/ Eyes hypnotic/ The way she moves those hips so damn erotic/ I can't get enough of her voluptuous body/ fuck with my girl have me catching a body/ I love my

Sugar sweet/ we argue kiss have sex and make Peace!"

As everyone danced to a new beginning. Peace had other plans. As Sugar dropped the hook, Peace checked to make sure if The Specialist was recording, "You got that, right?"

"Damn straight," replied the Specialist as he rocked to the beat.

As Sugar and Assassin came out of the booth everyone clapped except for Guns, Peace broke up the cheers and announced. "Let's Get it will be Assassin's first single,"

Guns never liked Assassin and always knew that Assassin was going to be a problem. Assassin would always spit his little rhymes for Peace. Guns never paid attention to Assassin nursery rhymes. He always wanted to kill Assassin so he could be next in line to run the show. Guns looked at Peace all up on Assassin's tip. He wondered how long it was going to take until Peace found out that Assassin wasn't real? Without speaking to anyone, Guns left out of the studio and got into his 2014 Audi. He reached into the ashtray and pulled out a blunt mixed with weed and crack and started to get high. He thought about how good it would feel to fuck Sugar Sweet in the ass. He whipped out his penis and started to jack off.

After a long night in the studio. Everyone hit the Hut out by Jamestown. Peace noticed every time Yolanda's cell would ring she would step to the ladies room. Sensing something wasn't right, he dapped everyone up before leaving. He hopped into His Range Rover and called up Goldshay. They met up at the Days Inn on South Main. Goldshay parked her Acura and got into his vehicle.

"Hey, baby." She leaned over and kissed his cheek.

"What up, ma. Take this money and go get us a room." He glimpsed at the short mini dress she had on and said to her, "Hurry up." He watched as she sped off to do what he asked her.

In room 319, Peace took a seat on the bed as Goldshay wiggle out of her tight mini dress. Peace liked Goldshay because she was straight to the point, he thought as she slid down to his hard erection and unzipped his pants and started to bless him. "Damn that feels good," He said as his cell began to ring.

"You want me to stop?" She asked.

"Nah, keep doing what you doing Ma." He answered his cell. "Who calling?"

"Me, Trish,"

"damn,you got a big dick," Said Goldshay as she shoved Peace's cucumber sized dick down her throat.

"Who is that?" Trish barked after hearing a woman's voice. Peace held his finger over his lips for Goldshay to take it easy on him so he could talk on the phone. "It ain't you," Peace responded as Goldshay pushed him back on the bed and started to ride him nice and slow.

"I need some money," Trish whined. "Come over here so we can talk."

"So now you wanna talk," Peace said nonchalant.

"Peace, I'm sorry for what I did to you. I keep having these nightmares about the abortions. I need you to help me get through this."

"Put that phone down, baby." Said GoldShay purposely,

"Peace. I know you not having sex while you on the

phone with me. Who is it.?"

"Damn, Ma."

"What?" Trish asked.

"I said I'ma get at you tomorrow." Peace ended the call and then flipped Goldshay over in the doggy-style position and started to fuck her nice and fast, strong and hard until he lost stamina, climaxed and fell on top of Goldshay with his pipe as deep inside of her as it could go.

"Damn, baby," Goldshay moaned as her body started to flutter from a great climax.

Peace woke up the next day and looked over at Goldshay's naked flesh. Shorty could do it all night, he thought as he got out of bed, dressed and crept out the room without waking Goldshay. He had a very important meeting with this guy named Nicks that Just was going to introduce him to.

Peace got into his ride and drove to his crib. He took a hot bath, then got dressed. He tossed on some Dolce & Gabbana jeans, a white-T, and some brand spanking new Air Force One sneakers. He went and sparked up a blunt and called Just.

"What up Playboy?"

"Ready to get this money. Meet me in front of my crib at a quarter to eight tonight."

"A'ight," Said Peace.

Peace met up with Just at a quarter to eight just like Just had told him to . When he pulled up front to Just's crib, Bree was in the driver's side of Just's all red Hummer, Just was on the passenger side. Peace parked and got in the back seat of the Hummer with Goldshay.

"Hey, Peace," Goldshay smiled.

"What up, Ma?" Peace spoke as he climbed into the back seat. As Bree drove them to the designated meeting grounds, Peace inspected his .45 Ruger just in case shit didn't go as expected." You sure this guy is cool?" asked Peace as he slid in his extended clip.

"Yeah, he good. But better safe than sorry." Just tucked his 9mm into his groin area as Bree pulled into an empty text tile building.

"You ready?" asked Just.

"No doubt," said Peace as he tucked his gun in his waist. Everything seemed normal thought Peace as he scoped out his surroundings.

"Grab the bag and let's do this,"

They got out of the Hummer and approached Nick's and his bodyguard. Nick's resembled the singer Ceelo Green. He was wearing a tailor made suit propped up against his limo smoking on a Cuban cigar like he owned the world and everything in it.

"What up, you bring the money?" Peace questioned.

"Who's your boy? This shit isn't cool," Nick's barked. "I thought we agreed no new friends. I have too much riding on this to be going to jail behind some nigga I just met,"

"Hold up. This is my manz, Peace. I don't do shit without him and you know how much I hate rats. Now apologize to my manz before shit gets heated," Stated Just as he pulled out his gun.

Nick's held his hands up in defeat. "I don't want no trouble. Any friend of yours is a friend of mine," Nick's reasoned.

Just said. "Glad you see things my way. Now let's talk like we have some sense. You got the money?"

"Yes, right this way," Nick's handed the bag of money over in exchange of coke.

"Nice doing business with you," Just remarked.

As Peace and Just made their way to Just's Hummer, Just said, "see how easy that was?" Peace stated, "Piece of cake," even though he kept having this funny feeling after serving

Nick's punk ass. Nick's was a piece of shit and the only reason he chose to do business with such a slime ball was because they taxed the shit out of him. Now all Peace had to do was call his supplier so he could get some work.

Roberto was the only one on his mother's side of the family who Peace could turn to when times were hard. The rest of his family wanted nothing to do with him because he was half black and not a hundred percent Dominican like them. Some people just couldn't get over that color barrier. Thought Peace as he made his way out of the crib.

He pulled up to his uncle's mansion in his SUV and was led through the tall metal gate by Jonny, the head of security.

"What up, Peace. He's expecting you."

Peace nodded his head and drove through the gate, as he drove up the paved drive way and parked. he took a deep breath hoping him and his uncle could come to some type of understanding. His uncle wasn't letting him grow. no matter how much money Peace tried to spend, his uncle would insist on giving him work on consignment. Maybe this time would be different, Peace figured as he grabbed

his brief case and exited the vehicle. As he approached the mansion, one of Roberto s body guards tried taking the brief case out
of his grasp.

"Nah, I got this," Peace said snatching his brief case. "Raise up." Peace gave Roberto s body guard a chilling stare.

"Sorry , but I gotta see what's in the bag. Now hand it over before you get smashed," said the huge body guard.

"Oh, yeah. " Peace punched his uncles body guard with a blow to the nose. As the huge man bled and moaned, Peace went to the door and rang the doorbell. "What up, Frankie?"

"Peace, for God sakes, what happened?" Frankie the butler asked as he looked at the bloody security guard. "He'll be right with you. I gotta get him a towel before he chokes on his own blood," Frankie said shutting the door behind Peace and running to aid the staggering body guard.

While Frankie helped his uncle's protection, Peace waited on the most powerful men in the game. Ten minutes later Frankie lead Peace to Roberto s back yard. As soft jazz played and Roberto danced with a lovely white girl who couldn't seem to keep her eyes off of Peace, Peace took a seat that Frankie lead him to.

"Go fix us a drink mommie," said Roberto tapping Paris on the rear before excusing her. He then went over to his nephew, Peace. Peace was like a son to him and the one who would be the head of the family's business if anything was to ever happen to him. Roberto smiled like a proud father and greeted Peace with a hug. "You're more than welcome to stay if you like," said Roberto as he observed the briefcase, "Just don't bring your hoodlum friends around." He had heard all about how vicious Q-Infinity was, so he reminded Peace. "It's good to have a clique in your line of work, but always remember to watch the ones you eat with. Trust no man and always go with your heart. Now that we got that out of the way, we can take care of business. You got that money for this week?"

"That and then some, uncle Roberto. I got your money and a million in cash. I thought I would show you that I'm not just depending on you. I thank you for putting me in a good situation but it's time for me to start buying my own product. "

"How dare you insult me after all I've done for you!?" Roberto asked furious. "So you ready to be big time, huh? When I was your age I was sitting on close to thirty million. The only difference is that I didn't have any help doing it. Why must you get greedy? Don't I treat you fair? I mean you got nice cars, money, and the type of life that most people would dream about. What's the reason to rush things?" he asked Peace.

Peace understood where his uncle was coming from. He responded, 'Tm thinking this game doesn't last forever. You treat me damn good if you ask me. You were there when no one else was. That's why I would rather you get this money before I let someone else get it, uncle Roberto. I Came to you like a man." Peace stated.

"And you will leave like a man, a rich man," Roberto assured. "Now come on. Let me introduce you to the new lady in my life." Roberto introduced Peace to Parris. "Don't worry about a thing because I'm going to send you so much coke that you will have no choice but to take over." He told Peace.

Meanwhile, Guns was tired of Peace's shit! Where was the nigga at anyway. Guns had been without coke for two freaking days. He was tired of the many customers beating down his door asking him if he was straight. that he left the spot and went to a strip club called Cabaret in Greensboro, NC. After spending nearly a "G" stack and not getting lucky, he became frustrated and left. Back in his city of High Point. Guns rode around in his Audi in search of a prostitute. He was all in 007, Commerce, Franklin, Green Street, Furlough. But ended up finding a nice stacked, dark brown skin sister standing in the Wu Wash location. He flicked his headlights. Moments later he watched the girl strut over to the car. She was wearing a short mini dress that accommodated her long legs, and a top that catered to her full double- D breasts. Guns dick was harder than a five cent jawbreaker when shorty walked up on the driver side of the car.

"Can I help you,"

"Get in." Guns told her.

Once she got inside the car. Guns pulled off and drove to a dark alley with a bunch of abandoned buildings. He parked and cut off his headlights, unzipped his pants and whipped out his dick, "Handle your business,"

"Are you sure we cool? I don't want to get jammed up," she said looking around for cops.

"yeah, we cool," Guns stated , "Suck daddy off." He was finally about to get some pussy. He was making progress, he thought as shorty went down on him.

Tonya was scared of the size of his gigantic dick size but she put his fat crotch in her mouth and gave him her famous blow job. She worked her jaws and moved up and down as she glared into his eyes. She was more than happy to get some pipe of his statues. She should've been the one paying him. He wasn't too attractive, but he was packing pipe like a porno star, she thought as she sucked and sucked until he burst. She swallowed every drop of him and didn't let a drip drop on the floor. She watched his head drift back in his seat and wiped her face and said to him, "Since I didn't make you cum in five minutes like everyone else, this one is on the house."

She tried to open the door and get out of the car, but he grabbed her by the hand and stopped her.

"You sexy as hell, ma. I really wanna try to see if you can handle me. I pay good," he said pulling out a large bank roll of money.

"Are you serious? It ain't all about the money. You made to suck not fuck big boy, and anyways I don't have any condoms."

"Don't worry, I wont cum in you." He pulled her onto his lap.

Tonya lifted her skirt up a little and climbed on top of him. Boy was she gonna pay for this later. She squinted her eyes as she rode Guns. All she could do was hold onto his neck as her head banged on the roof top. "Stop, please stop," she begged.

Guns could tell shorty didn't really mean stop. He ripped through her until he could no longer hold his nut. He crammed every inch of his twelve inch dick in her wet slit and let go.

Gun kept stroking rotating his hips as she took all twelve inches of his pipe. Tonya forgot how much pain she was in and rode him until she climaxed. She had one orgasm and was working on another. Her body started shaking and her legs started trembling as she enjoyed another great climax. She tried to get up when she was finished, but he held her down and kept pumping away until he shot into her.

"Damn," she said as she hopped off of his lap.

"What's wrong?" Guns asked as he stroked her moist vagina with his index finger. She moaned and then let out, "You don't have to pay me. I need a break." She grabbed his hand and pulled it from between her burning thighs. "You got a big ass dick, you know?"

Guns laughed. He liked shorty. So what she was a prostitute? Maybe if he held her down she would leave the streets alone. "Come home with me."

"I would but I have to work. I can't leave my post," Tonya said with a sigh. Didn't he know that she was a trick and nothing more, and that she had a job to do, plus an expensive coke habit. Without her consent, Gun pulled off. He got to asking questions and found out that her name was Tonya. He drove to his trap spot and he and Tonya chilled there the whole night.

The next day, Guns took Tonya on a shopping spree. He bought her some fly gear, got her nails done, toes did, and paid to get everything she needed to enhance her beauty done. At the end of the day his lady was looking like one of America's Next Top Models. Guns was excited to finally have his very own dime piece. It just went to show what a little money and tender loving and care could do. Now the only problem was everyone kept checking Tonya out, which was a problem cause Guns was extremely jealous. When they left Four Seasons mall, Guns schooled Tonya on his pet peeves.

Number one, no prostitution. Number two, never fuck around on him. Number three, never disrespect him around his boys under any circumstances. Number four, always look her best when in the public eye. "Understood!" Guns asked as he pulled off in his Audi. Not only did Tonya make Guns look good, but she made him feel like a real beast. It was time for him to make some real money and be the boss! Even if it meant stepping on Peace's toes. Guns went and picked up four bricks from Peace, then called up one of their nemesis.

"Yo, Cash. This Guns. I heard you guys were without work."

"Who told you that?" Cash snapped wanting to know how the fuck Guns got his number.

"I just took your boy Chip some work. I got some sweet deals for you. You know it's a drought and I can give you three of them things for twenty a piece. Maybe if you deal with me a few more times, I might drop the price a little."

"Where we need to meet? I really need them three big boys from you. Maybe when my people get straight we can work something out," Cash asked.

"Yeah, cool. Meet me at the Do Drop Inn on Centennial street in thirty minutes. Don't be late," Replied Guns.

Cash hated fucking with off brand ass niggas, but coke

was scarce. The bad part about this all was his little foot soldiers were going behind his back copping coke from just about anyone. This really bothered him. Maybe he could start a partnership with Guns until his connect got straight. Cash parked in front of Club Do Drop Inn and waited on Guns. When Guns rolled up in his Audi, Cash got out of his Beamer and stepped to Guns vehicle. He had to give Guns credit where it was due. Guns had a fine ass bitch with him. Cash got into the back of the car and exchanged a bag of money for a bag with three kilos in it. He poked a hole in one of the kilos and tasted the product. "That's good shit."

Cash said as his nostrils flared up, "I can't feel my face. That's good shit. Yo, Guns, you think you could get me ten of these things for a hundred and fifty thousand. My man hasn't called me in a couple of days. I don't know what the fuck is going on.

"Maybe I can get you ten for two hundred the way things are right now." Guns handed the bag of money over to Tonya. Call me back in a couple of days and we might be able to work something out," said Guns.

Cash despised the Q-Infinity clique, but he had to deal with them since they were running shit right now and his connect Roberto was out of coke for the moment. Cash drove to his mansion and bagged up coke. He then took Chip and the crew some work. Prices were higher, but they didn't seem to mind as long as they had work on the strip.

While Assassin got interviewed by 102 Jamz radio host Akima, B-Daht, Big Mo, Brian B, Roxie, Chris Lea, and the entire 102 Jamz staff. Assassin was proud that his single (Let's Get It) had reached such decent numbers. His new single was getting so much spin on the radio that is was almost impossible to walk the streets without people knowing who he was and wanting his autograph. He was a star in the hood and things couldn't have been better. He gave Peace the nod as he wrapped up his interview.

After the interview Assassin and Peace went to this bar called Sharkey's, a lounge that everyone migrated before the club. Upon walking in the crowded lounge, Peace spotted Trish out the corner of his eye. As usual, she was rocking her looking for a baller outfit.

Trish noticed everyone looking at Peace and Assassin and made her way over. "Come on, Shay. I see my boo." She tugged Shay by the arm. When they reached Peace. Trish held out her hand. "I need some dough, cream, chips, money, gwop, whatever you call it," she snapped as she held out her hand expecting a blessing.

She had him fucked up, Peace mused. "I don't have any paper on me right now, Trish." He said to her as he patted his pockets.

No this nigga wasn't trying to play her. Trish tried telling herself." "Assassin can let you borrow a few hundred and you can give it back to him."

"Don't do this." Peace hated Trish's guts ever since that abortion she had." Get the fuck out my face before I stomp a mud hole in your ass."

Trish got in Peace's face causing a scene. "Nigga, you ain't built like you think. Don't nobody need your money anyway," she snapped. "You broke ass nigga. I hope somebody robs your bitch ass."

"Fuck you, hoe! Open them legs and spread love, bitch."

"Oh no you didn't." Trish said feeling hurt by Peace's words.

"You nasty, dirty dick ass, no fucking, eating pussy ass, no paper having nigga." She said before she stormed off.

Meanwhile, Cash, Chip and the rest of the Southside gang sat afar as they caught what went down between Peace and his girl. Trish. Cash knew this was a good time to make his move, so he paid the bartender to take Trish and her girl a drink. Like Clockwork they made their way over.

As Peace and Assassin shot pool, Chip made his way over to their table. Not wanting to be bothered, Assassin ignored Chip.

"Eight ball in the corner pocket. Yeah," Shouted Assassin as he collected his money from Peace as the eight ball sunk into its hole.

"What up, Carlos?" asked Chip as he laughed.

"Not right now you whack ass nigga. I don't feel like it tonight. Fall back," said Assassin.

"I just wanted to get at you and show everybody in here just how bitch you are," remarked Chip.

Assassin socked Chip right in his big mouth without any explanation causing him to hit the ground. Peace grabbed Assassin and they made a break for it before they caught a major beat down. Both men ran until they were out of breath. They ducked behind an old trash can in an alley as a gang of angry Southside niggas gave chase. Out of breath and slumped over, Peace laughed. "You crazy, son! You about to get us killed. You know we wasn't packing heat."

"I know but I'm tired of that fool. I couldn't take that shit anymore so I decked him. I think I broke my damn hand when I hit that fool." Assassin shook his hand which was burning with pain.

"Peace chuckled. "Let's be out while we can." They climbed a fence and headed back to Irving Projects.

***

Money, power, respect can get you anything in life. After getting Peace's bitch Trish pissy drunk, Cash talked her into ditching her girl. He couldn't wait to fuck his enemy's girlfriend. He had big plans lined up. He parked his car at the Holiday Inn and went and got a room. He placed his hand around Trish's waist and lead her to room 460. Inside of the room, Cash kissed Trish and rubbed the gap between her thighs. He couldn't wait to tell his crew how he banged Peace's bitch.

"Hold on," Trish sat up from the bed and said. "You know
the drill, Cash. If you plan on getting up in me I need some security," said Trish stretching out her hand.

Cash went into his pocket and gave Trish ten hundred dollar bills. He placed them in her hand. "Since I helped you mommie, see if you can help me. " Cash dropped his pants to his ankles.

Trish placed the money inside her pants pocket and went down and blessed Cash.

CHAPTER 9

Assassin was too caught up in his fame to realize that Sugar was carrying his child. Yep, Sugar had been feeling sick so she went to the hospital and found out that she was pregnant.

"Damn! This can't be happening to me. Why me? She thought as she walked into her apartment and took a seat on the sofa. Today was really a bad day for her. What should I do? Do I tell Assassin or do I let him do his thing? She didn't want to be the one to mess things up for Assassin. He was doing so great in life with his music, so how was she just going to up and say, I'm pregnant? I'll probably sound like some type of groupie chasing after his money, she thought. "Damn, damn, damn, fool. You always make bad choices." She laid on the sofa and started to cry. She was so caught up in her misery that she didn't hear the knocking on the door. She heard keys rambling and Yo-Yo's voice as she used the key Sugar had given her to get in. Now Sugar regretted giving her girls a key to her apartment. She tried to dry her eyes, but Yolanda was on it.

"What's wrong with you girl. Why you crying? It's gonna be okay," Yolanda assured her girl while patting her on the back and embracing her. After no comment, Yolanda knew something was awfully wrong. "Did Assassin hit you?" Yolanda rose to her feet. "I'ma kick his damn ass. Come on, I'll teach him to put his hands on you." Yolanda started for the door.

Sugar grabbed Yolanda by the arm. "No! He didn't hit me. He would never hit me, so stop tripping." Sugar wiped her teary eyes.

"I don't believe you," Yolanda said unmoved. "Stop protecting him. Let me know what's going on. You my girl, you can tell me anything."

"Damn. I'm pregnant, okay? Don't be mad at me. I' know what I gotta do," Sugar crossed her arms together.

"Yeah, me too," Yolanda thought." Come on, Sugar. I'm not mad at you. Did you tell Assassin about this?" She questioned. "I'm sure he's going to help you raise your baby. Clean up your face so you can roll with me to get something to eat. We can talk along the way."

"I thought we were going to get something to eat? Why are we in Irving Projects?" asked Sugar getting suspicious.

Yolanda pulled in front of Peace's building. "Come on, I got to get some weed from my guy right fast, come on," Yolanda said as she parked and got out of the car. She lead Sugar to a group of guys. "Shorty, can I speak with you for a second?"

"No doubt. Any friend of Peace are friends of mine." Stated Shorty.

After talking to Shorty, Yolanda was able to find out

which apartment Peace was in. She knew if she could find Peace then Assassin wouldn't be too far behind. She lead Sugar to the apartment Shorty gave her. Yolanda tapped on the door and a girl with perfectly round breast and half her ass showing answered. At first, Yolanda thought she had the wrong address until she saw Peace and Assassin. Assassin was on the couch puffing herb like everything was alright when it wasn't, She hated him for taking her Girl Sugar through this unnecessary bull crap.

Assassin got up and turned the music off when he saw Yolanda and Sugar at the door. He knew something had to be up.

"Come on, Assassin. Why you turn off the music? That was my jam," Cried one of the girls they had over as she stopped winding her hips.

"Yeah, but my girl come before all that shit!" Assassin explained to the girl that wanted to hear the rest of his CD. Assassin walked over to Sugar and placed his arm around her and kissed her long and strong. "Sit down," He told her as he took her over to the sofa, where she sat down, he asked her, "What's wrong, you should've just called if you wanted to see me."

"I'm sorry, boo. I know how busy you are. I didn't want to worry you," Sugar said as she searched her purse for tissue as tears slid down her face.

"It's alright, ma. I'm just happy to see you.' He kissed her lips and wiped her tears away.

"If you so happy to see her then who all these girls? Niggas ain't nothing," spat Yolonda as she rolled her eyes and despised the skank bitches Peace and Assassin had in the spot. "Tell him what's up so we can get the fuck up out of here so they can do their thing. "

"Tell me what?" Assassin looked at Sugar and hoped he didn't give her no STD's.

"Tell him before I tell him,' Yolonda threatened. She peeped Sugar wasn't going to say anything. Her girl was getting weak for this nigga. She was so mad Sugar wound up pregnant. They had so much money to make, and so many more niggas to rob. "She pregnant," Yolonda blurted out. "it's yours and you gonna take care of it so don't try no bullshit. " To Yolanda's surprise, Assassin picked Sugar up and swung her around like some shit out of a fairy tale.

"I'm gonna be a daddy. Peace, you gonna be a god father," Assassin celebrated.

Sugar smiled like she was ready for marriage. Yolonda hated this. She knew right away she had lost her girl to Assassin. Damn all of this was such bad timing. Sugar couldn't be too happy about the two girls in the crib. Yolonda had to put an end to all the celebrating. "Sugar, you should be pissed the hell off about these girls over here. He's a dog like the rest of them. Dogs run in packs. " She looked over at Peace and sucked her teeth as he talked to one of his raggedy heffahs. "Yeah, I said it, nigga. You ain't shit. You want me to sweat you but you not even worth it. I'm glad I got a real man now. Are you coming or staying here with these out of date hoes?" Yolonda asked Sugar.

"She staying here with her baby's father. Thanks for bringing her over here, but let me tell you one damn thing; I don't need you brainwashing my girl with that foolishness," Assassin said as he wrapped his arms around Sugar to show Yolonda who was running the show.

"Cool," spat Yolonda. "And don't come crying to me when he shits on you. I won t be trying to hear that shit," she told Sugar.

"Good," Assassin said as she stormed out. "Get the fuck out,"

Yolonda left. She couldn't believe Sugar picked a man she barely knew over her best friend. At this point she had no words for Sugar.

Assassin had moved into Sugar's apartment. Hell, he was even paying all of the bills, being that he used her crib for a stash spot. He had been spoiling Sugar to death with back rubs, foot massages, and strawberry sherbet ice cream. Not only was the sex great with Sugar, but he loved her to death.

Assassin got into his Tahoe after making sure Sugar was strapped in good. They were leaving the Greensboro coliseum after watching a Tyler Perry play.

"Damn," Assassin uttered out as he watched Trish and Cash walking to Cash's Beamer hand in hand. How was he going to tell Peace. Assassin kept his glance on Trish and Cash as they tongue wrestled.

"Baby, what's wrong?" Sugar asked. "You just cursing for no reason,"

"My bad, ma. You see shorty?" He nodded to Trish.

"Yeah, and?"

"That's Trish. She use to fuck with Peace. You see that nigga she with,"

"Yes," she replied.

"He's no good. Trish can cause a lot of drama behind this type shit. Niggas in Irving Projects can't stand niggas on South Side. Him and Peace don't get along to save they life! Trish is one dumb ass broad. Cash be on that rape shit,"

"For real. Maybe you should go see if she's okay," Stated Sugar.

"Nah, let that bitch learn," he said before driving off.

Assassin pounded into Sugar as she shook from an orgasm. She flopped onto the bed as her legs began to tremble. Assassin had broken her off a little something something. As she laid across the bed, Assassin got up, grabbed his cell and went into the bedroom. Sugar got up and tiptoed to the bathroom so she could eavesdrop.

"Son, she was with Cash. Yeah, I'm sure. All you gotta do is give me the word and he's finished. I can handle Cash, and let Angella and Terra beat the shit out of Trish."said Assassin.

"Nah let that shit ride. They already in enough shit as it is. Plus a hoe gon' be a hoe and a nigga gon' be a nigga." Peace stated.

"You sure you don't want me to get Terra and Angella to kick Trish's ass. She disrespecting our set fucking with that lame," Assassin said in frustration. He wanted to get Terra and Angella to run down on Trish, beat her ass and then maybe cut her face up , because they could fight but they were better with a razor, "To bad they were locked up." Assassin thought to himself.

"Nah, don't worry yourself."

"I ain't,' replied Assassin. "One." He hung up his cell

and took a deep sigh. His manz was getting soft on him. He thought back to a time when Peace wasn't always so humble.

Assassin dribbled his basketball wanting to be like one of the NBA greats. That's when he saw Peace and two niggas giving him hell. Assassin wasn't the smartest kid in the world , but smart enough to know that some shit was about to go down.

"Aa! little nigga. Burn the road up. How many times do I Have to keep telling you, you can't pump in these projects. Ever," stated Bobby Steal.

"Who were they to tell him where he could pump at? Peace kept selling the work he got from his uncle Roberto. After his mom past away last week, he said fuck the world and started hustling. He knew Bobby Steal and Killer all too well. They had ran him off the strip numerous times , Peace felt like fuck it today, He ignored them which caused them to get even more roused up.

Bobby Steal tapped Killer on the arm and said to him. "I'm tired of talking to this nigga. I'm about to kick this niggas ass one last time. These my projects ," Bobby shouted out.

"Don't go to that nigga. He got some garbage. I got that fire," Shouted Bobby Steal. He didn't like the fact that a new kid in their neighborhood was taking his customers. "These my projects, " Bobby claimed. He started shouting out loud drawing a crowd. "I'm about to show this nigga who he dealing with." Bobby Steal and Killer approached the tall lanky kid.

'This makes the third time this week we don't kicked

your ass. How many more times I have to tell you. These my projects." Bobby Steal shouted.

Peace sat on the green radiator and watched Bobby run his fucking mouth. "Nah, you ain't whoop my ass cause you can't fight your way out of a wet paper bag. Killer the one who's been kicking my ass. One on one I will knock you out," Peace challenged.

Everyone was outside that day. Guns, Crook, Just, 45, Tyshawn, Rico, Lil Love, Malik, Harlem, Smoke, J-Hood, Big boy, Hot Jit, Heavy, Murder, Skee Mask, Big B. Earl Nelson, lakim, Lamont, Damien, Yonah Bey, Jr, Chris. Everyone in Irving Projects was there that day. Including Trish.

"So what you saying?" Bobby asked even though he just heard what the kid said.

"I said give me a one on one. If you win I promise not to come back around your stomping grounds, ever! But if I win you give me my respect," requested Peace.

"Around here you gotta earn your respect. You know how long I've been running shit around here," Bobby Snapped. "Let's get this nigga." Soon as Killer moved, Peace pulled out his chrome Desert Eagle and put two in his wig. Then he approached Bobby Steal. "You ain't shit without your homeboys." Boom, boom," Needless to say, Assassin never wanted to be an NBA great. He wanted to be a made man like Peace. Word. He loved his nigga to death, but was worried that if they didn't set some examples pretty soon, niggas would start thinking they was pussy.

Sugar ran and got in the bed, she prayed that Assassin didn't do all of what he said on the phone. She pretended to be sleep as Assassin kissed her. No man had ever loved her the way that he loved her. To think she was six months into her pregnancy stages. Shit was too good to be true. It's like she was living in a fantasy, except she wished Assassin would leave the game. She often waited and worried about him many nights. It was time for him to start thinking about his responsibilities, because he was about to be a father soon. As he wrapped his arms around her body she asked, "Do you love me?"

"And you know I do," he replied. Planting soft kisses along the nape of her neck.

"Will you leave the game for me and the baby? I mean, we need you more than the streets. Plus you saved up a shit load of money. You all I got. Cherry and Yolonda won't even speak to me because I chose you over them. I need you to tell me you'll stop hustling. I need that from you, not the nice clothes or money. I need you to be here for us, Bae" she kissed him.

"I promise, ma. I'm just gonna do the rap thing." He took Sugar in his arms. They made love into the wee hours of the morning.

CHAPTER 10

Weeks had gone by and Yolonda was still up to her old ways. She had Cash kicking out money like a slot machine. The good part about that was she hadn't even came out of her panties. True she wished things between her and Peace could have went better, but life goes on, she didn't need him or Sugar for that matter. She checked out her appearance as she glimpsed in the mirror. No one could touch her in her tight Prada dress and heels. She left out the house and jumped into her Benz and drove to the Motorcycle club. A large club on near downtown High Point. The line was thick and she would've had to wait forever if it hadn't been for Peace, who tapped her shoulder.

"What up, source money? You coming with me or waiting in this long ass line?" asked Peace as he glared at Yolonda' s sexy body and caramel complexion.

She knew she was wrong for messing with Peace, but she followed his ass anyway. It felt so good to be with him again. Peace led her straight to the dance floor where they started to groove. They danced for a couple of songs until he started palming and caressing her rear end. "Hey, player. Watch your hands. " She moved his hands up to her waist and they slid back down to her rear. She didn't bother removing them, she just wrapped her arms around his neck and grooved to the beat.

"Check that bitch out," Chip said to Cash as they chilled at the bar. "Isn't that Jasmine over there with Peace? Don't tell me yall messing with the same girl," spat Chip. "This some R. Kelly and Usher shit. You better put your foot down," warned Chip.

"Let's bounce," said Peace to Yolonda.

"Let's not. I have to go meet someone. Thanks for getting me in the club." She waved as she stepped off.

Cash was pissed the hell off. Especially after Chip pulled up on him about Jasmine. To think he was tricking all of his doe on this high class ho!

"Hey, bae?" Yolanda walked up and gave Cash a kiss on his lips.

"What up with you and that nigga Peace? You feeling that nigga? I can hook yall up," asked Cash in his body, (feelings).

"I don't want you to do nothing, bae. I'm here with you." She rubbed his broad shoulders to keep him calm. And whispered in his ear. "So stop making a scene." She kissed him softly on his cheek.

"Yo, your girl over there with Cash." Just nodded to Yolanda. "How you let that slip away."

"Fuck that broad." Peace said. "It's plenty more bitches in the sea." Everything he did Cash tried to duplicate. Cash wanted to be him so bad. He wanted to piss Yolanda off, and at the same time show Cash up. He stepped to this tall exotic sister that favored Garcelle Beauvais that use to play on the Jamie Foxx show.

"Excuse me miss, can I get a minute of your time?" asked Peace.

"That depends on what you talking about," She threw back. Damn he was fine! She thought as she took a sip of her alcoholic beverage.

"You leaving with me."

"You straight to the point aren't you? I admire that. I am ready to leave. I caught a taxi here so I could use a ride home." she said.

"Come on. I brung an extra helmet. I hope you like motorcycles." asked Peace as he took her hand and lead her out the club. He could see Yolanda breaking her neck to look at who he was leaving with. He could tell she was steaming hot, but fuck it. Once outside, Peace got on his Kawasaki and started the engine. "What's your name and where you live?" asked Peace as she placed on the helmet he gave her and climbed on the back of his bike.

"D, and I live in a suite at the Radisson Hotel,' she answered as she held on to him tightly.

Peace pulled off as his engine roared. He couldn't help but to show off a little. He bust a wheelie and weaved through the North Main Street traffic.

D held onto the smooth gangster she just met. If he played his cards right, there was no telling what the night could lead to. She leaned up against him as the cool breeze brushed against her honey brown skin.

Peace flew through traffic like a bat out of hell until he

got close to the Radisson hotel, where he slowed down and pulled up front. He let her climb off the back of the motorcycle and killed the engine.

'That was so fun!" said D, as she took off her helmet.

"We gonna have to do that again," she giggled.

"For sure," replied Peace as the valet boy ran up.

"Need your keys, sir."

D waved, "Hello, Travis."

"Hey, Ms. Wells. I'll park that for you," said Travis. Peace looked at the young teen and gritted. "Yo, don't scratch my shit homeboy."

"I promise not to." Travis reached for the keys.

"I'm telling you, homie," Peace threatened.

"I know. Don't scratch your shit," replied Travis, grabbing the keys and hopping onto the motorcycle.

"Come on," she took Peace's hand.

Peace followed D, too busy watching her precious long legs and petite frame to notice what she was saying.

"You didn't hear a word that I said." She stopped and smiled.

"What was that?" Peace questioned.

"That must be some good weed you smoking on," she laughed.

"For sure,"

"I hope you have more of that," said D as she used her key to get in her apartment.

"Yeah, I got plenty." he stated.

"Then roll up while I go get us something to drink on." D went to the bar and tried to decide what she had a craving for. Hennessey. Nah, Grey Goose, nah, Long Island tea, nah. She went for Jamaican rum. That always got her twisted. She grabbed two wine glasses and went to the freezer. She put ice cubes into their glass and went into the fridge and grabbed a bottle of A&W Root Beer and mixed it with rum.

She went in the living room where Peace was rolling up a fat spliff. "You know you look like the rapper Nas?" She gave him his drink.

Peace smiled. "I hope that's a good thing."

"I think he is so sexy," stated D.

'Thanks then. I take it that you model since you have so many pictures of yourself." Peace looked around as he lit up the spliff and took a big gulp of his drink.

"Yeah, does that bother you?"

"What bothers me is a shorty as fine as you. I know you gots to have a man," Peace remarked, passing her the spliff.

"No man," she could honestly say. "I prefer it that way.

"What made you leave with me. I could've been some psychopath?"

"I needed a ride home. And besides, you don't look like a psychopath." She passed the blunt, chuckled and rubbed his cute face. "You look like the type that will only hurt if you had too." She held his face and stared at him. Damn she couldn't wait to get him undressed. "What's your name by the way?"

"Peace," He leaned in and kissed D before she could ask another question.

"Hold it." She broke the kiss. "Who was that girl you was dancing with at the club. Are you using me to get back at her?" D asked seriously. "She was gorgeous."

"Not as gorgeous as you. And let's not worry about her tonight. Let's just focus on you and me and what we have right here." He dumped the blunt in the ashtray and commenced to kissing D again.

She kissed back with urgency. He scooped her up so that she was mounted on his waist. "First room to your right," she
entertained him with kisses as he carried her to her bedroom. "Get undressed. " She started helping him come out of his shirt, once his shirt was off, she unbuckled his belt, unfastened the buttons to his pants and slid them down to his ankles.

Peace spilled his drink as he lifted D's shirt up over her head.

"Ahh! My carpet." She whined.

"Shit. My bad." Peace laughed as he stared at D's round B-cups.

"What." D asked insecure of her breast size. She knew she had twice as much ass as she had breast.

"Nothing,' Peace said as he pulled her up against his hard pipe. "You sure you wanna do this," he asked.

"Why?" asked D. It had to be the girl she had seen him with at the club. "Why you getting all scared now? You wasn't scared when you asked me to leave with you."

Peace sort of laughed to himself. Shorty had spark. "Nah, I ain't scared , ma."

"Then shut the fuck up and go with the flow." She came out of her Diesel jeans, kicked off her heels and stood before him in a lime green with black laced Victoria Secret set. She shoved him onto the bed. "Got condoms?"

"Nope," he knew he had forgot something. It's not like he was scared to fuck shorty, but real talk. It's like they came from two different worlds. Him a hustler. Her a sweet, innocent and naive model.

"Boy." she snapped. Then went to the night stand and pulled out a fresh box of condoms. "Strap up." She threw a box of Magnums his way.

Peace caught the condoms and strapped up as D unsnapped her bra and came out of her panties. She walked over to him and took him in her embrace and they began to kiss each other frantically.

"Lean back and let me do me," said D, as she straddled Peace and entered him into her. She arched her back and gyrated her hips and began to ride him with a nice slow tempo. Peace just laid back and enjoyed the ride. Somewhere along the way of their love making he must've drifted off, because he pretty much didn't remember anything but the smell of eggs, toast, and turkey bacon the next morning.

"I made you breakfast and coffee," said D placing a tray with Peace's breakfast on the nightstand beside him. She was almost late for her photoshoot, so she rushed to put her earrings on.

"I've got a photo shoot I have to go to. You can stay and just lock up before you leave.

She gave him a peck on the cheek and said, I really enjoyed last night."

"Then let me know how to keep in touch." Replied Peace.

"Just leave your number on the night stand. I have to go.

My taxi is waiting," Said D as she hurried out of her hotel suite.

Peace ate breakfast, got dressed, and left his number on the nightstand.

***

Things were better now that Assassin had stopped hustling. Now Guns was the next in line. Sure Crook was tight with Peace, and had just as much coke as him, but the only problem was, Since Guns had been dealing with Cash charging him outrageous prices, Crook hadn't been moving as many birds for Peace as he had. Thanks to Cash, Guns had been moving like four kilos a week. Since Peace and Cash hated each other, Cash had to go through Guns if he wanted to cop. No one but the Q-Infinity gang had coke threw out the city. Not only did they have shit on lock, but anyone who was dealing had to come to them to get work. They were making a killing. Too bad Peace was seeing most of the money? Thought Guns. Now if he could only find a way to move Peace out the way and really get things popping. But
first he had to figure out a way to take out Assassin first so he wouldn't be seeing and hearing his name so fucking much. Swear to God he kept hearing that niggas name all over the place. Assassin this Assassin that. Everyone was hyping that clown up like he was like that when he wasn't. He was straight pussy. Sure his single was gold , almost platinum, but he was still bitch in his eyes. Guns looked up at Tonya as she cooked dinner in her Victoria Secret lingerie set. As he counted his money, he thought about all

the bitches who had been try'na get with him. Not only was he fucking the shit out of Tonya every night, but he was also fucking fly bitches on the regular. Who's ugly now thought Guns.

Money was coming in hand over fist. Coming in so fast it was hard for Peace to keep tabs on it. He was selling coke sky high and no one was complaining since coke was so hard to come by. Since his uncle Roberto had cut off most of all the top suppliers in Peace region, Peace was really starting to see some heavy decimals. Things were going well for Peace. So much so that he started a small record company called Ty Productions. So far Assassin was the only artist signed to the label, but pretty soon, if an went well, he could sign a couple hot new artist.

He heard about some cat's called Tragedy/ Bobby Kocaine and the Rachet boy crew. O.G Wall was doing big things, Uncle Durt, Mass Appeal, Mike Lucus, Jadone Success, John Monk, Vic Qwest, Chad Wayne, Guilty County, Caliph Stafford, Fate, and a bunch of other talented artist.

(Let's Get It In) was quickly climbing up the charts doing record numbers. Besides being on his grind and the music thing. His relationship with his girl D was going better than he could've hoped for. At first he didn't think they would ever work out because of their different paths of life, but he was dead wrong. D could care less about his rough background or past. She just loved him beyond measures. Shorty was unlike any woman he had ever dealt with. She was supportive and she actually cared for him and his well-being. Often they would sit up in the wee hours of the morning talking about how each other's day had gone. She would hip him on what happened in her world, and vice versa. He would fill her in on what was going on in the streets. She didn't stress him , neither was she after his money like most women he had came encountered with. D was independent and he loved that about her. Damn. he was pussy whipped. He smiled as his cell chirped, it was a private call. He never answered private calls, but today he was in a good mood. He accepted the call.

"Peace speaking,"

"Baby. I'm running late at my photoshoot, can you come and pick me up so we can still be able to go out to eat? You remember where you dropped me off at this morning?" D asked. "Yeah. I'm on my way."

"Love you," She said to him.

Peace drove up to Market Square where D was working and parked up front. It wasn't long before D walked out with her coworkers. A bunch of beautiful ladies approached his SUV.

"Peace, these are a few of my friends; this is Sara," said D. Sara needed no introduction because she took the initiative to introduce herself.

"Hi, I'm Sara." Sara smiled and held her hand out for Peace.

Peace smiled back. "What's good Sara?" Sara was white and from the way she was looking at him she was probably fascinated with black men. He shook her hand, but she just kept gazing at him with her light blue eyes.

"He's cute. Why didn't you tell me you had such a good

looking man?" asked Sara.

"Cause I know you got jungle fever and I would hate to jump on you girl, stated D.

Everyone started laughing Sara was cool ,but she wasn t the type to leave around your man. Sara had slept with any and every one to get to the position she was at now. Not that she wasn't beautiful, it's just when she was around a good looking guy , her panties just couldn't seem to stay on, "Nyisha, this is Peace. Peace. this is Nyisha," D introduced the two.

"Sup ," Peace nodded. "Are you ready?" He glimpsed at his Movado watch and saw that they were running late for dinner.

"Yeah, hold on," said D. "This is my girl Tiara, Amber, and Cassandra ..See yall later. We running late. He's taking me out to dinner. "

"Girl, aren't you gonna tell us more about Peace. Like what he does for a living?" asked Amber.

D hated the stares she was receiving. "He's a record producer.

You might know him. He produced the track on the radio called (Let's Get It)."

"Wow! " All of her girls were astonished. She wanted to smirk in Ambers' face for trying to put her on blast and for hating so damn much.

"Can you get Assassin's autograph for me?" Amber asked D.

"I'll see what I can do." She knew it would be a cold day in hell. "See you later." D waved as she climbed in the SUV.

"Those bitch's so damn nosy." She chuckled."Did you see their faces when I told them you produced Assassin's hot new track?" She giggled and cut up the radio. "Talking about getting her an autograph, you get it yourself, ho," she spat.

Peace shook his head and drove. As he glimpsed in his rear view mirror he saw a police car following. "Damn," he said to himself as the police hit the sirens. He pulled over to the right side of the road. It was his worst nightmare, Officer Wolf. He couldn't stand the white son of a bitch. He hated the blue eyed motherfucker. Wolf approached with caution, gun in hand and his finger on the trigger.

"If it isn't Mr. Vanchez? You know the drill, license and registration, ma'am. Stay calm. I'm going to need your I.D. What are you doing with this piece of shit? You do know he's a gang member and a low life motherfucker, don't you?" Wolf asked.

"That low life motherfucker is my boyfriend. What's the reason you stopped us for?" He just picked me up from work. That's it." D spat, hoping to God Peace didn't have any drugs in the car.

"S.W.A. sister with attitude. This asshole was swerving like he was drunk. Now get out of the vehicle."

"I'm calling my lawyer," spat D.

"Chill." Peace calmed D down. She was wilding the fuck out and he didn't want her to get caught up in any of this drama. He emerged from the Rover with his hands up.

For the first time since they had been together she was scared for Peace and the life style he chose. She watched as he got hand cuffed and tossed onto the jeep. She wanted to say something, do something. She couldn't stand to see the cop roughing Peace up with brutality.

Officer Wolf's eyes pierced threw Peace. His 6ft4 body lingered over Peace as he searched his pockets. He found no drugs, just stacks of money in every one of his pockets.

"That's a lot of money you got on you. I'm gonna have to seize it until you can come up with some check stubs. This is how it's going down. Every month we meet up, I want five thousand. If you re late on your payments you'll be seeing me on the regular. You catch my drift? As long as I'm paid I'm happy. The way my wife spends money is driving me freaking crazy. I gotta do something while you drive around in your flashy little rides, with your sexy little women." He shoved Peace into the SUV.

"I'm not a big drug dealer like you, Peace. I got a respectable life. See you next month around this time. Tell Ms. Wells I loved her in the new juicy magizine," said Wolf as he took the cuffs off of Peace's wrists. "You 're not under arrest yet, but you will be in a little while. Now get back to your destruction," said Wolf laughing all the way to his squad car.

Peace climbed into his SUV three thousand dollars shorter. If Officer Wolf thought he was just gonna rob him and get away with it, he had another thing coming. Seemed like everybody wanted a piece of the crop these days. Instead of police trying to lock him up they were willing to turn the other cheek as long as they got paid. That didn't sit well with Peace. Five thousand a month, kiss my ass, he thought until he looked over at D.

"So what happened, because he didn't write you a ticket

or anything? So when where you going to tell me that you sold drugs. "It doesn't even matter, just keep that shit away from me," she spat. "You know you don't have to sell drugs and we can still make it, Peace. I don't care about money and nice gifts. I would rather have you. I don't wanna have to visit you in Central Prison . But I will cause that's just how much love I have for you. I don 't know what I would do without you." She planted her hand on his face and glanced at him in a serious manner.

"Don 't worry. I wont ever leave you for nothing in the world. " Replied Peace.

"I hope not," Stated D. She loved Peace with her everything. She just wished he would get out the game so they could start building a future together.

Chapter 11

"Boo, I'm tired of waiting. Take them clothes off. I been fucking with you too long not to hit that ass, ma. I been wining and dining you. I spent about thirty stacks in the last month on you and you ain't even showed me no tits or nothing, bitch. Get right," spat Cash. "I'm tired of being nice to your ass."

Cash pulled out his gun from his waist line and sat it on the dresser drawer.

Yolonda was shocked at the turn of events because up until now, she thought Cash was smooth and laid back. Damn, why did she forget to bring her gun? She asked herself. She was slipping and way off point. But she wasn't going out without a fight thought Yolonda as she broke out and ran. She was quickly apprehended by Cash who shoved her so hard that she slid across the wooden floor. Her heart was racing so fast that she didn't even realize that her elbows were bleeding until she glanced down at her dress. She kicked and screamed as Cash lifted her up by her hair.

He threw her over his broad shoulders and carried her to the room, where he tossed her onto his bed, laid her face down, lifted her dress, tugged her panties to the side and crammed his large penis in her anal.

Yolonda thought she was gonna pass out and die as Cash sodomized her. She tried not to cry but tears swept down her eyes as he ripped through her brutally. She screamed and begged for him to stop but he didn't, he kept thrusting his hips and moving in and out of her violently. Yolonda tried gyrating her hips to make him hurry up and climax, she yelled and fought as he pushed deeper and deeper into her. She was relieved when he finally ejaculated in her. That only excited him more.

"You like that don't you. You freaky little bitch." He began to plow inside of her even harder than before.

Yolonda couldn't remember what happened after that because she momentarily blanked out. When she reopened her eyes, Cash pulled out of her anal and entered her vagina.

"Damn this shit's good. I see why you got Peace nose all open. That nigga could never hit this pussy like me. Never." Cash plowed in and out of Jasmine viciously.

"Stop! Please stop! ." Yolonda tried kicking and shoving Cash but he was just too strong to be moved.

Cash began to beat Jasmine furiously. "Bitch, bitch, bitch.

I really liked your ass. And Peace, watch what the fuck I do to him." Cash beat the fuck out of Jasmine and got up after he climaxed. His covers were soaked with blood. "Stupid bitch." He kicked her. "You got my new sheets bloody. I'll be back to deal with you later. You re one dead bitch," said Cash as he looked at Jasmine's unconscious body.

Yolonda laid on Cash's bed stiff and bloody until she decided dying like this wasn't going to be her fate. She knew if she had any chance of living then it was going to be now
or never. With all of the strength she had she used it to get out of the bed. She grabbed her purse, shoes and clothes and made a dash for it.

Cash hopped out of the shower and dried off, put on his clothes, lotion, and then went into his room. There was no sign of Jasmine. He ran to his surveillance cameras and saw her putting on her clothes then making a break for it. If this bitch told the police he was going to be in big shit thought Cash as he ran to get his gun. He shot out of the bedroom window recklessly as Jasmine hobbled over the fence. Damn. She was slicker then he thought. He tossed on his shoes, he was gonna kill that bitch once he caught her.

Yolonda dialed 911 on her cell phone as she ran down a dark country road. She was miles away from anything. She could hear the dispatcher asking her where she was before she fell to the ground in the middle of the street. The last thing she remembered was bright lights and car tires screeching. Was she finally about to meet her maker?

Mr. and Mrs. Hopkins rode on a dark country road in Archdale,N.C. on their way home from church.

"That looks like someone lying in the middle of the road. Stop!" Mrs. Hopkins told her husband who almost drove them off the road.

"My God," said Mr. Hopkins coming to a halt and

parking the car. "We better see if she's still alive. "

"I sure pray to God she is," Said Mrs. Hopkins as they got out of the car to assist the lady in the middle of the road.

"She's still alive," said Mr. Hopkins.

"She's bleeding bad. We better get her to the hospital as quick as we can. I sure pray that she makes it," replied Mrs. Hopkins as her husband got the lady out of the middle of the street and in the back seat. Mr. and Mrs. Hopkins prayed all the way to the hospital asking God to have mercy on the lady's soul and to let her make it.

God must've heard their prayers. Assassin, Sugar, Cherry, Crook, and even Yolonda s mom who had driven all the way from Charlotte, N.C. was at the High Point Regional hospital.

"I hope she's alright. " Yolonda s mom Ms. Stephens said as she and Sugar stood awaiting news on Yolanda's status. "Can I see my baby?" asked Ms. Stephens as the doctor approached.

"You have to be immediate family," said the short Asian doctor. "I'm her mom and this is her sister," said Ms. Stephens.

"Right this way," said the doc.

"Oh my god." Ms. Stephens covered her mouth in shock. "Who did this to my baby?" She went to Yolonda s bedside and rubbed her hand. "Be strong baby. "

Sugar took one look at Yolonda and started to cry. "I can't look at her like this, Ms. Stephens. " She cried.

"It'll be alright. You have to be strong for her. Okay?" Ms. Stephens placed her arms around Sugar and lead her to

Yolanda's bedside. "She's tough, she'll pull through. "

"I'm sorry for not being there for you Yo-yo," Sugar said as she sniffled with tears in her eyes. "Please forgive me," she said apologetic. After no response from Yolonda, Sugar was filled with rage and wanted revenge to seek Yolanda's rapist. "I'm sorry Ms. Stephens,I can't stand to see my girl like this."

"I understand, I can't believe someone would do this. I want whoever that did this to her dead," Stated Ms. Stephens.

Sugar understood where Ms. Stephens was coming from. She also wanted them dead. "I'll be in the waiting room if you need me. I need to clear my head." Sugar said wiping the tears from her eyes and then leaving. She was beyond pissed off, she was furious. "Assassin." She said as she got in the waiting room. "I can't believe that Cash raped my girl. I'm going to kill that nigga! If it's the last thing I do. Take me to find him."

"Hold." Assassin rushed over to her aid. "Calm down. Now what's going on," he held her.

"Cherry said Yolonda told her she was about to go to Cash's place. He's not getting away with what he has done to my girl."

"Calm down. You know you're about to have my seed. Now you let me handle things and you chill here with Yolanda's mom." he hugged her and kissed her forehead. "I got this," He told her.

Minutes later Assassin was outside of the hospital calling up Peace.

** * **

D woke up from the sound of Peace's cell. It was driving her crazy. She reached over and grabbed his cell from the night stand and tapped him awake. "Your phone keeps ringing," she said handing him the cell phone.

"Yo," Peace said half awake.

"Son, where you at? I'm on my way to come get you. It's time to do some shit we should've been done did," said Assassin.

"Cool, I'm over at D's crib." Peace didn't know what was going on but he knew whatever it was had to be important if Assassin was calling at this time of the morning.

"What's going on? Who was that? It's two in the morning," D said looking at the clock that hung on the wall.

"I gotta handle some business. Aight, ma?" He gave D a kiss.

"Be careful," said D with worry.

"For sure." Peace got out of bed and got dressed. He tossed on a black hoody, jeans and boots. He grabbed his Desert Eagle and made his way outside where he waited in the lobby for Assassin. When Assassin and Crook pulled up in Assassin's Tahoe, Peace got in the backseat and didn't ask no questions. He just checked to see if his gun was ready for battle.

"Yolonda got raped by Cash. The doctors don't know if she's gonna pull through or not," said Assassin. "He beat her pretty bad. "

'Damn. " Peace felt like his heart was ripped out of his chest. Him and Yolonda had their share of quarrels but he never wanted anything to happen to her. He was ready to kill something. Anything. The more he thought about Cash raping Yolonda, the angrier he became.

Assassin looked in the rear view mirror at Peace's reaction. He hadn't seen his boy this angry in a long time. "It's time to kill this bitch ass nigga like we should've did a long time ago. He got my fucking boo upset crying and shit. I'ma make his momma cry," said Assassin.

"Word, I'm feeling that." Peace took a tote from the blunt Crook had passed him and tried to amp himself up for the killing spree that was about to take place. "Call up Guns,"

Assassin wasn't feeling Guns because deep down inside he knew he was dealing with a snake. "The quicker we kill Cash the better. I know where he might be at. I think he be hanging at that after hour joint called Conclusions. Let's check that out." Assassin suggested.

"First call up Guns and Just and tell them to meet us at Larry's apartment. The more fire power the better," Peace responded.

Assassin didn't agree with Peace's move but he called Just and explained to him what had happened, then last but not least, he called Guns. "Yo. Some shit just popped off and we about to meet at Larry's apartment,"

"Some shit like what?" Asked Guns as this chick named Delicious gave him head in the whip.

"Just meet us at the trap and I'll explain everything," Assassin suggested.

"Cool," Guns ended the call and guided Delicious down on his shaft. "Hurry up, ma. I gotta make moves,"

"Okay," spat Delicious with a whole lot of dick in her mouth. She bobbed her head up and down until she watched him stiffen up. Two minutes later Guns was kicking her out of his vehicle.

"How am I going to get home?" She wanted to know.

'The best way you know how. Walk bitch." He pulled off leaving the girl with dick on her breath. Guns made it to the PJ's in a little under five minutes. He went to Larry's apartment where the crew was preparing for combat. Gun's were everywhere.

M16, Mac-11's, AK 47s, Glocks, rifles, pumps, and sawed off shoties. They had all types of guns and ammunition. Only thing they didn't have for a war was grenades.

"What's going on here?" Asked Guns as dope-fiend Larry closed the door behind him.

"Cash bitch ass raped Sugar's home girl Yolonda and we're about to take it to him," stated Assassin. "Throw on a vest and get ready," Assassin said, tossing Guns an all black bullet proof vest. "Grab your gun,"

"Aight," Let me take a piss right quick," responded Guns. How dumb could Cash be? He made his way to the bathroom and called up Cash.

"Yo, son. How stupid can you be? You know Peace try'na kill you behind that bitch Yolonda?" asked Guns.

"I don't know no bitch named Yolonda. Fuck Peace. He can kiss my ass. I'll be damned if I let anybody do anything to Cash nigga. " Cash hung up.

"Hard headed mother-fucker. Die then. I was just giving you the heads up." The audacity of some niggas. Guns thought.

"What's taking that nigga so long?" Assassin asked Peace and the rest of the clique. "I'm about to go check." Assassin tapped the bathroom door. "Come on!"

Guns opened the bathroom door. He hated Assassin, especially when he tried to act like the boss. Who did he think he was ordering him around? Guns gave Assassin a look of pure hatred then said, " I'm ready."

The plan was to run into the Conclusion lounge and kill anything moving. They knew Cash and his crew would more than likely be hanging out at the all night lounge. Assassin drove as Guns, Crook, Just and Peace prepared their weapons for battle.

Guns had a 9mm riffle, Just toted the Mac-11, Assassin had a P-90 Ruger with extra clips, Peace had a Desert Eagle and 44 Magnum. And Crook packed the Ak-47.

As Cash got drunk and played a game of pool with his manz Lil Vicious and his crew grooved to the sounds of Mobb Deep, the Q-Infinity niggas crept through the front door unnoticed. Peace and Just led the pack, they started blasting and people scattered all over the place. Niggas ran for dear life and bitch's hollered, screamed, and anyone with good sense hit the deck.

While Cash and Chip made a break for it, scrambling for their lives, and returning fire at the same time, Assassin watched Cash flee behind the bar and reload his clip into his gun.

Cash shot wrecklessly trying to hit anything or anyone. He knew he couldn't be wasting any bullets if he wanted to continue to live. How am I gonna get out of this alive? He asked himself. God wasn't always there when you needed him but word up, he was always on time thought Cash as he grabbed one of his soldiers sliding across the floor. Cash pulled Mike close to him and said. "Cover me. "

As Mike let off shots, Cash ran for the exit. He looked back in time to see Mike take a shot to the head. Close call, he thought as he ran up the steps and dodged a bullet that grazed his arm and made him speed up his pace.

While Assassin trailed Cash, Guns, Crook, Just and Peace shot it out with Chip and the rest of the South Side gang.

Cash tossed an old lady on the ground to buy himself some time. Assassin held fire and helped the old lady to her feet and then pursued Cash. Little did Assassin know but Guns was hot on his trail. Cash climbed four steps at a time until he ran out of stairway. He lunged and kicked open the door that led to the roof top. "Damn." He was running out of room.

"Yeah, nigga got your bitch ass now," said Assassin out of breath. He aimed his gun. "This for Yolonda.

Cash stared at the long way down to the ground. Then leaped over onto the next building over.

Assassin was too late. He watched as Cash tumbled onto the next building over like a bouncing ball. He wanted to pursue him but was scared of heights.

"Fuck you Due Boy !" Cash gave Assassin the finger and was hit by a shot to the stomach. "Ahh. " he groaned in pain.

Assassin laughed before he was pushed off the edge of the roof from behind, Guns watched as Assassin tumbled to his fate. There was a loud thrashing sound and the people below were screaming. A part of him was relieved. Now all he had to do was break the news to Peace.

"You alright?" Guns yelled out to Cash.

"I got shot. Does it look like I'm alright?" Cash yelled , covering his wound with his hand to stop the steady flow of blood that was gushing from his stomach and oblique area.

Peace, Just and Crook did all the destruction and killing they could do. Bodies laid on the floor ready to be sorted out. They were running out of ammo so Peace called them off ."Come on, let's bounce."

As they fled the scene, shots rattled like the Vietnam war. "Yo, Where Assassin and Guns?" asked Peace as they made
it out of Conclusions.

"Assassin didn't make it," Guns said with fake tears playing his role to the tee. "Cash killed him before I got there. I'll tell you about it. Come on before the cops get here," said Guns.

"He fell off the roof ," Someone said as a group of people huddled around Assassin's lifeless body.

Peace took one look at Assassin's dead decapitated body and his heart beat stopped. Just had to literally drag him to the car that was parked out front.

"I should've got there a little sooner. Cash killed him before I could get there. I think I shot Cash though. I don' t know," Guns put on as Just placed Peace in the back seat.

"What you mean you don' t know if you shot him?" Peace raised his voice. "You was supposed to have his back." Peace snapped.

"Yo. Just intervened. "We all loved Assassin. He was that dude. Real niggas don't die. They live on!" Just could feel Peace's loss. He leaned over and placed his arm around Peace as he mourned Assassin. "We're all hurting," responded Just.

As Sugar sat at Yolonda s bedside with Yolonda s mom, Ms. Stephens at the High Point Regional Hospital. Peace came walking into the room dripping wet.

Peace felt he had to be the one to tell Sugar what all went down. How could he face this woman, let alone tell her that Assassin got killed. He hated himself for allowing this to happen. He looked at Sugar and then at her round belly. Damn. This was one of the hardest things to do in life. He took a deep sigh.

"Peace. Tell me you and Assassin got who did this to her." Sugar glimpsed at Yolonda s swollen eyes and bruised cheeks.

"Peace what's wrong, why are you crying?" she asked sensing something wasn't right. "Did I say something wrong?" She asked as Peace broke out in tears. Sugar opened her arms and gave Peace comfort. "What's wrong. Tell me."

"Assassin got killed."

"What. how. He can't be." Sugar shouted in disbelief. "I can't believe this. No, no, no! This can't be happening to me. Assassin isn't dead," Sugar said before she fainted.

Peace caught Sugar before she could hit the floor. "Can you help me out with her?" Peace asked Ms. Stephens.

"Oh my God." Ms. Stephens rushed to aid Sugar. She rocked Sugar in her arms. "Everything is going to be okay."

"Sugar cried. She felt like her whole world just crumbled. "How could you let this happen?: Sugar yelled at Peace.

"It wasn't my fault," Peace replied.

"To hell it wasn't," Sugar hissed.

"Now Sugar," Ms. Stephens intervened. "I understand that you love Assassin," She sympathized, "But that doesn't give you the right to take your anger out on him. Sorry, but this had been one hell of a night." She apologized. "Peace is it?" she asked.

Peace nodded his head in response, "yes ma'am."

"You really look like you need to get out of those wet clothes and maybe get some rest. This has been a rough night for everyone." Stated Ms. Stephens.

"I can't. I have to find who did this. Look at Yolonda, and what about Sugar? Her child will never get to know it's father. What am I supposed to do," he questioned.

"Put it in God s hands. I understand that you loved your friend, and I see the genuine love you have for my daughter. I understand that you're worried about Sugar, but eventually Sugar will get through this, and Yolonda will get better. Now can you please go get some rest for me and get out of those wet clothes you have on."

Peace smiled for the first time that night. Yolonda's mom was sweet sort of like the mother he once had. Peace left the hospital thinking of all the lives he had fucked up. As the rain poured down, Peace hitched a taxi and got the driver of the taxi to drop him off at D's crib.

D laid in her bed asleep when she heard the door being opened. She knew it was Peace. She got out of bed and found him on the balcony. "Baby, it's cold out here. Come inside and take off those wet clothes. Is everything okay." she inquired.

"Shit is far from okay. Assassin got killed, and now his baby momma is blaming me, and to make matters worse this girl I know got raped."

"Do you have feelings for this girl?" Asked D.

Peace shrugged, "I don't know."

"As long as you recognize where home is, It's all good. Now let me help you get out of those wet clothes," D said. She helped Peace get undressed, tossed his clothes in the washer and then ran him hot bath water. "How does that feel?" she wanted to know as she massaged his neck. "Peace, I've been thinking. I want you to get out of the game. I need you and I don't want anything happening to you! I make enough money so that we will be financially straight. What will I do if something was to ever happen to you?"

"It ain't easy. Just pray for me. It's crazy right now!" Peace took a deep sigh.

"We can move to New York or Atlanta. I have money saved up. I can find work over the internet. My agent has been trying to get me to move for the longest time." D tried compromising.

"Baby, it ain't going to happen." He got out of the tub, dried off, and through on his boxer briefs and went to lay down in the bed, leaving D in the bathroom.

After being shot in the stomach, Cash ran to seek help. He had lost a lot of blood thanks to that little punk Assassin. He was about to tap on one of the tenants who lived in the building when he felt light headed and passed out. He woke up in the hospital in a hospital gown, and knew he had to get the hell out of dodge before Peace and his crew launched an attack. The pain was unbearable, but yet in still he climbed out of the bed and made it to his feet. Once on his feet , he made his way out of the hospital. It was cold outside and he was walking around half naked. There was only one person he could call, and that was Chip. He approached the telephone booth and roughed off an old lady for her quarter. "Can't you see I need to use the phone lady!"

"What about my quarter." The old lady asked huffing and wheezing from tussling with the young street punk.

"Charge it to the game old heffah."

"God don't like ugly. I wish my Teddy was here, he would teach you a lesson, you ole punk." The lady said as she walked off.

Cash shut the door to the phone booth and ignored the old lady, placed his call and told Chip to come and pick him up. Ten minutes later, Chip pulled up in his Yukon Truck. He laughed as Cash got into the ride. "What the hell happen to you," Chip inquired, staring down at the slit in Cash's gown.

"You don't want to know, hey nigga. Watch your eyes." Cash fixed his gown and said to Chip, "Drive me to my place."

***

"This is a sad day in Hip Hop. Rapper Carlos Newmen a.k.a Assassin. was found dead this morning. From what I hear he tumbled to his death at 4:30 AM. Police don't know if it was suicide or foul play. He will always be remembered for (Let's Get It). He will be missed by many. And now a moment of silence for my man Assassin." DJ and radio host Roxie, of 102 Jamz said paying her respect to Assassin.

D and Peace made their way to their seats as the Reverend started his sermon. It was the day of Assassin's funeral, and D had talked Peace into letting her attend the funeral with him. She felt she had to be the one to help him get through with losing his best friend. Peace took a look around and saw Sugar, she was wearing a black dress, gloves, and a veil. Right beside of her was Yolanda, who was out of the hospital, and Yolanda's mother, Ms. Stephens. They looked wonderful as well as everyone else who came to show their respects to Assassin. There was so many people who came to show their love and support. Peace was glad that he had given Sugar the money to take care of the funeral arrangements because she did a heck of a job with everything to make sure that his homie got a proper burial.

"Rejoice cause Mr. Newman has gone to a better place called Heaven. I understand that Carlos was expecting his first child with his child's mother, Sharmane. They say when God takes someone out of this world, someone else is born. Carlos was loved and he certainly will not be forgotten. Our hearts go out to Sharmane, as well as his family and loved ones.

Peace watched Sugar cry and Yolanda give her comfort. Just that quick all hell broke loose.

"Not my baby, oh God no. Not my baby." Everyone was bewildered because no one even knew that Assassin even had a mother.

Peace gazed at the Charades. This had to be a fucking publicity stunt. Who was this woman screaming her baby this her baby that. Assassin's mom was too busy smoking crack to take care of her thirteen year old son.

Assassin's mother really stole the show when she broke down in front of the alter and asked , "God, why my son?"

Peace had seen enough. He was about to get up and put an end to all the craziness, when D. patted him on the leg. He was glad he had brung her along, or else he probably would've ruined what was supposed to be a good day.

After the funeral, Peace approached Just, Crook, Guns, and the rest of the crew. The whole Q-Infinity clique was like forty deep. Peace was so deep in conversation that for a minute he forgot all about D. As he started yapping, he noticed D talking to Sugar and Yolonda. That was definitely a no, no, "Get at y'all in a minute," said Peace, excusing himself.

"You must be Assassin' s girl friend? I've heard so much about you. Sorry about Assassin, and if there's anything Peace and I can do for you or for the baby just name it," D said to Sugar.

"You're?" Sugar asked , extending her hand out.

"D. I'm Peace's girlfriend." She introduced herself and then stared at the girl next to Sugar. She was gorgeous even with a bruised lip and blemished eye."And you're ?"

"Yolonda"

"I've been looking all over for you. You ready to leave?"

asked Peace.

"I was just talking to Sugar and Yolonda. I was letting Sugar know that if she needed anything to let us know. I saw you talking to your home boys so I made my way over here," stated D.

Yolonda looked at Peace for the first time since her release from the hospital. He was so handsome in his all black suit. She couldn't fault Peace for finding someone new after how she screwed up with him. She couldn't say that it didn't hurt seeing him with D, cause it did bother her just a little bit because in her heart, she still loved Peace.

It wasn't a day that went by that Yolonda didn't think about Peace. The roses he had sent to her while she was in the hospital, and the I love you cards didn't help either. Seeing him with D made the possibilities of the being together slim.

D wrote her number down on a piece of paper and gave it to Sugar. For the first time in a long time, she felt insecure. Yolonda was hard to compete with. She was amazingly beautiful.

"I will give you a call if I need anything." Sugar scanned the number and said, "Why don't you all come to my place. I'm having a get together and I would like it if you and Peace came,"

"We would love too. Wouldn't we Peace," she asked.

She sure put him in an awkward situation, Peace pondered as he glimpsed at Yolonda. "Sure we can swing by and show our respects."

"I didn't know she was Assassin's mother," Sugar

grabbed Peace by the arm and they made their way over to the puny old lady. She had Assassin's features, his same brown skin and chinky eyes. You could tell she was Assassin's mother. The only bad thing was she was dressed terribly. Her hair wasn't made up, she had nappy cornrows, corduroy pants, penny loafers shoes, plus a dingy sweater.

"You must be Carlos's mother." Sugar held her hand out.

"Yes I am. And you are?" she asked, shaking the young ladies hand.

"My name is Sharmane, and Carlos and I are expecting a child together," Sugar explained, rubbing her belly in small circles.

"Don't tell me I'm going to be a grandmother. Carlos was always the surpriser. That boy sure made good for himself. I read about the funeral in the High Point Enterprise. I wonder why no one had contacted me." Assassin's mother looked at Peace.

"I don't know why either, probably because he never mentioned you before. Now all of a sudden you show up at his funeral. Did you hear he was making some money and decide to be a mother?" Peace spazzed out.

"Now, Peace. She has a right to be here. It's good she came. I'm glad you're here," Sugar said to Assassin's mom. "And I would like for you to ride in the limo to my place afterwards." Sugar tugged Peace's arm and walked with him. As they made it to Assassin's grave site, Sugar looked at Assassin' s tombstone. "Peace, I miss him. I can't stop thinking about him. I want Cash dead, he has caused so many people grief. I want him dead even if I have to kill him myself. I know Assassin didn't slip and fall. Doesn't that sound crazy to you?"

"Especially when he was scared of heights. I know something isn't right. Give me some time to find out what's going on, and I promise you that nigga Cash is dead when I catch him. "

"Good. I want him to hurt like I hurt." She wiped her teary filled eyes with tissue.

"Yo. Now I see why my manz wanted to leave the game and settle down. He had everything he needed in you," said Peace.

Sugar smiled "I know you think I hate you, but I don't. I was just upset about everything that happened. Now I see why Assassin looked up to you. He really loved you." She gave Peace a much needed hug, and said, '"Peace, I'm serious. I think the only way I can have this baby and sleep at night is to know that Cash is not , in existence. I don't want him to harm anyone else." She wiped her eyes.

Peace held Sugar tight. "Don't worry. I told you I will handle it," said Peace.

After Peace got finished talking to Sugar, he went and found D. As they headed to the car Guns approached. Peace opened the door for D, let her in the Rover as Guns walked up .

"What up, my G?" Peace asked.

"I don't know," Guns removed his shades and wiped what appeared to be tears from his face. "I don't know how many more funerals I can take. "

"Me neither," was Peace's response. "I'm about to turn some shit upside down."

"Right," Guns agreed.

"Well," Peace took a deep sigh, "Get at you." He gave Guns a brotherly hug. "Yo, I think your girl waiting on you."

Guns glimpsed back at Tonya and caught her checking Peace out. "Yeah. You know how it is," Guns stated. "But yo, let's get up and do business. We can't let a minor setback stop us from getting this money."

When Peace arrived at Sugar's crib, everyone was there. Crook and Cherry, Yolonda and her mom. The whole Q-infinity entourage. Yolonda s mom had prepared the food. The whole crew just chilled, mostly talking about old times. Everyone was laughing as Crook, Peace and Just started telling stories about them and Assassin. Damn they missed their manz and them like hell. Sugar just enjoyed all of the stories. Peace knew deep down inside she was hurting. She had been through so much, and he didn't want her stressing, it wasn't good for her since she was in the late stages of her pregnancy. She looked as if she could have the baby at any moment. D was glued to Peace's arm, and Yolonda just kept looking over at him periodically. Peace wanted to be there for her, but how could he. He loved and wouldn't hurt D purposely, but still had deep feelings for Yolonda.

"Peace, can I speak to you?" Assassin's mom asked.

"For sure," Peace got up from the sofa and went to talk to Assassin's mom and was happy to get out of the awkward situation that he was in.

As they got into the hallway, Assassin's mom began to speak. "I know I was a bad mother, and I thank you for making sure Carlos was okay. I know who you are. I remember when Carlos used to stare out the window looking at you with all that gold on. I knew it would only be a matter of time before he chose that lifestyle" She wiped her eyes wishing she had been a better mother.

Peace felt sorry for her, but how could she leave her thirteen year old son in these mean streets?

"Carlos was a good kid. Smart in school, and the boy was so wise to be so young. I know how much he hated me. He didn't always hate me, you know. Well, not until I got on drugs. I started selling my body, leaving him home hungry, and all because I wanted to get high on drugs. I never got to tell him how sorry I was and now he's gone," she cried.

Peace had no choice but to embrace the foul smelling old lady.

Sugar came over, smiled and then they all had one big group hug. Peace had to break things up before he shed some tears. "It's getting late and I need to get going," stated Peace, glimpsing at his Movado watch. He told everyone goodbye and him and D bounced.

***

"Bye, mom. See you tomorrow. I'll be alright," Yolonda said to her mother as her mother left, giving her a kiss, then Sugar, and waving goodbye to Assassin's mom.

Yolonda had helped Sugar clean up everything after everyone had left. She knew Sugar had been through a lot. For some strange reason Yolonda couldn't stop thinking about Peace and how she had fucked up with him. Seeing him with D only made things that more complicated. How did she go from sitting on top of the world to the bottom of the barrel? She hated Cash and wanted him dead. He raped and violated her in the worse way. Every time she looked at herself in the mirror, she got all depressed. Not only did he hurt her physically, but mentally as well.

She couldn't believe she slipped the way she had. All she could think about was the torment he put her through. If it hadn't been for her will to survive, she would be dead. She knew the Creator had spared her life. Thinking of that dreadful night, tears started forming up in her eyes. She stepped in the bathroom to conceal her pain, she cleansed her face and got herself together before going to get her purse.

"See you tomorrow. I'm about to head home, you want me to drop your company off?" Yolanda asked.

"Are you ready to go home? You never told me your name?" Sugar asked Assassin's mom.

"Lily, and I guess I better be leaving. I have to be at the shelter before nine tonight, or else they wont let me in."

"We better hurry up if you trying to make it," replied Yolanda.

"See you later, Sharmane. I'll come over tomorrow to make sure you are okay." Lily took a deep sigh as she got up from the couch.

Sugar felt bad for Lily. The least she could do was let her stay and make sure she had clean clothes and a bath. She needed some company.

"I have a guest room you can stay in and extra clothes, and I don't want to stay by myself. I can take her to the shelter tomorrow. Yolanda, you just head home and call once you get there."

"I'll do that. Bye girl." She gave Sugar a hug, and said goodbye to Ms. Lily.

After Yolanda left, Sugar showed Lily to the guest room and gave her some cosmetics, undergarments, and clean clothes. That night Sugar had cried herself to sleep thinking about Assassin, and how she was going to raise their child without him.

***

Guns was a star in the hood. For the first time in his life bitches were trying to holler at him. He had the money, power, now all he needed was the respect. He knew he should've felt bad for killing Assassin but he didn't. Money outweighed a friendship that never was.

With Assassin out of the way he could use Peace to become one of the largest drug lords the city has ever seen. It was only a matter of time before Peace slipped up, and when he did, Guns would kill him just like he did Assassin.

He pushed Tonya up off of him as she slept and got out of the bed. He wiped the sleep from his eyes and sniffed a line of coke. This caused Tonya to wake up out of her sleep, she crept up behind him, hugged him, kissed him. took the hundred dollar bill from his hand and took a sniff of her own. She then got on all fours.

That was the thing he loved so much about Tonya, she had a mean head game, he cuffed her head and guided her to his serious erection. After getting one of the best head jobs in the world, he lit a Newport cigarette and called up Cash.

"What's good, boy-boy! I haven't heard from you in a minute. A little flesh wound didn't get you shook did it?"

Cash replied, " Picture me being shook. I just been trying to heal up. Word on the street is that y'all closed down shop?" Cash's objective was to pick Guns for information.,

"That's why I was calling. I got like two kilo's left if you want them. Peace kind of shook after that thing that happened with Assassin and all and I don't know the next time I might be straight. "

"I feel you. I can take them off your hands. I got in touch with my connect and he said it won't be long now. You know I can give you twice as much as Peace is giving you. That's if you your own man, which I know you are," Cash questioned.

"You know me? I'm about my paper. I was thinking about getting rid of Peace so we can really start to see some paper." Guns wanted to get Cash to team up with him and then rock his ass to sleep! Fuck a team when he could run shit himself.

"That's what I'm talking about, playboy! So where you want to meet up at?" Cash asked. "Give me a couple of hours and I'll let you know." Guns ended the call.

Chapter 12

Crook pulled up to the curb in his 2010 dark colored blue Chrysler 300 on 22 inch rims and parked

"Wait here," he told Cherry as he got out of the driver's side of the car.

The block was filled with nothing but family. Milk, Lil Love, Rico, Smoke, Harlem, J-Hood, Heavy, Hot Jit, Murder, Astrop C Rize, Brandon Mayor, Murder, Charles, Vick, Big B, Earl, Lakim, Free, Fred, Elliot, Andre, Relleo, Atari, tellas, Brooks, Shawn, Nino, Scoobie, James Miller, Bear, Just, Plus Angella and Terra, who had just finished up 18 months in jail for multiple counts of inflicting serious injuries. Terra and Angella are two of the sexiest, most dangerous females on the face of the earth. They were looking damn good. Crook reminisced about the days when Angella and him used to have a thing going on. That was before Terra moved into the neighborhood and stepped on the scene. She had fucked Angella's head up before he could get the snatch. For those who don't know what that is (pussy). Angella could be so innocent, sweet, feminine, and easy to handle, but her girl Terra was a whole different story. She was tomboyish and not feminine at all, plus she was mean as all outdoors.

Crook dapped up everyone in the crew before making his way to Angella. Angella would put you in the mind frame of Keri Hilson. She was tall, petite with firm tits, and a perky ass.

"Sup, ma." he flirted.

"The rent." Terra butted in, rolling her eyes and crossing her arms. "He ain't shit," she mumbled to no one particular.

"Say, what's up with that funky attitude?" He focused his attention on Terra. Terra looked a little bit like a brownskin Jennifer Lopez. She was a dime piece but her attitude made her something like a seven or six, Crook reasoned.

"What's up with that funky bitch in your ride?" Terra glimpsed at the girl on the passenger side of Crooks vehicle.

"You lucky I don't go kick that off brand bitch ass." Bringing other hoe's in their project was a sign of disrespect.

"Stop hating. You know what you need?" he asked with a smirk written on his face.

Terra responded. "No, maybe you would like to tell me." She walked up to Crook, crossed her arms and gave him a challenging stare.

Crook gripped his genitals." Some pipe in your life." Before he knew it, Terra had pulled out a razor on him and in return he had pulled out his chrome 44 Magnum on her.

Just intervened before things got out of hand. "Chill

out!" Just told Crook," Y'all are click."

"Word." Crook set his pride aside and lowered his gun. "Sorry about that. Sometimes you can be a real bitch." He puckered his lips and blew Terra a kiss to get under her skin.

"Eat me," Terra spat. If there was ever something she hated it was an arrogant ass nigga, and that's what Crook was. A conceited, self-centered son of a bitch. "I hate you!" she blurted out.

Just said to Crook, Angella and Terra." Can you all cut the bullshit out? Look, Peace wants to speak with all of you. So stop the bickering. What are you going to do about shorty?" Just nodded to the girl in Crook's ride.

"Hold up." Crook went to the car and broke Cherry off a nice stack of money to do some shopping.

"Love you, bae." Cherry kissed Crook's lips then got into the car and drove off.

"Come with me," Just said to Crook, Angella and Terra.

"Do she love you or your money." Terra asked Crook on the sly.

Crook stopped. He and Terra needed to have a one-on-one.

"Look, what is it about me that you don't like?"

"You want the real?" Terra asked. She sighed deeply. "Everything about you. You conceited as hell and every word that comes out of your mouth is nigga this, or bitch that, and I really hate how you treat me in front of everyone. You should learn how to treat a lady."

"Is that right?" Crook stroked his goatee with his index finger and thumb. "Maybe you can teach me," he said, glimpsing Angella's ass from a distance.

"Maybe I can. And just for your info, I'm not gay," she spat.

"It is what it is," replied Crook. That wasn't what he had heard.

Terra couldn't believe Crook thought she was a lesbian. "Strickly dickly." She glimpsed down at his private region. "What is it about me you don't like?"

"First off, you not feminine," he stated.

"Whoa." This was news to her.

"Let your hair down, buy some new gear, recognize a boss when you see one."

Terra laughed. "You're not a boss."

"But I will be someday," Crook fantasized.

Peace swept Angella up off of her feet and gave her a bear hug." Where Terra and Crook."

"You hurting me," Angella laughed. "They're probably airing it out," she said once he placed her back down on solid ground. "I hope they don't kill each other. Why didn't you come and visit us?" Angella asked Peace.

"I don't do jail." He meant that literally.

She could understand that. "At least you kept money on our books. You know I ate good in that hell- hole," she teased.

"No more of that fighting and shit. Time is money. Plus I have a special assignment for you and Terra."

"What is it?" She was anxious to know.

"You'll have to wait until everyone is here," Peace said as Terra and Crook walked into the apartment. He lifted Terra off of her feet and gave her a bear hug like he did to

Angella then let her down on solid ground. "You two have to promise not to get into any more trouble."

Both girls knew that Peace loved them without a doubt and cared for them like a big brother would his two sisters.

"We won't, Peace," they said in unison.

"Good cause I missed the hell out of y'all." He gave both of them a hug to show his love and affection.

"We missed you too," Angella said , "So did you ever find out who killed Assassin?" Assassin was more like their younger brother so of course they wanted to ride for him.

"No, but Guns said it was Cash." Peace paused , thinking about his dead homie.

"You can't believe Guns. That's one cruddy ass nigga," Terra started yapping.

"Show 'nough," Angella agreed.

"That's clique," Just butted in.

"Yeah, but he still ain't shit," Terra blurted out.

Peace agreed with Angella and Terra, but until he had actual proof , he didn't want to assume because he hated assuming shit. Sooner or later Guns would slip and he would be there when he did. Peace wasn't the smartest nigga in the world , but he was observant enough to know Guns was selling too much coke for one man alone. And so he set his plan in motion. He looked at Crook. Crook was one of his most loyal soldiers.

"You know the word on the streets is Guns outselling you like 5 to l," Peace stated.

Crook could see Angella and Terra laughing at him. "Yeah, but I make shit go smooth around here. Chasing niggas down for money they owe you. Never once has your money come up short. And if it did, ain't a nigga around who can say they owe you a dime. I bust my gun."

Crook thought about all the niggas he had bodied in the last year for Peace. "And if you look at the spots that got robbed , Guns was in charge of those."

"So you think you can do better than Guns?" Peace asked. "With my hands tied around my back and eyes closed." Crook gave an arrogant smirk.

"Good, cause I need you to hold shit down while I get some things in order," stated Peace.

"What!" Terra butted in, "I'm not dealing with nobody but you." She rolled her eyes at Crook. The two of them had bad history and it was no secret.

"So what the fuck is you saying, Peace. You just gonna leave us out to dry?" Angella couldn't believe what she was hearing. Crook wasn't built to be a leader. He was a soldier and nothing more. Strong, but lacked leadership skills.

Peace finalized all arguments. "Either deal with Crook or not. It's up to y'all. I would hate to lose y'all but I made my decision. "

"You know Crook is going to have us on the block competing with them thirsty ass niggas out there." Terra looked out the window at Milk, Lil Love, Rico and the rest of the crew as they ran up to cars.

"I told them about that shit," Crook said to Terra with a smirk on his face.

She was going to hate dealing with Crook. She had been so focused on moving up the ladder, and to have something like this happen was like the ultimate demotion. It was like going from sugar to shit. She had to try one more time. "Peace, you know Crook is too bossy , self-centered , too mean, and not fit to be a leader. He will probably start us off with looking out." Which was the lowest position of the crew. Sort of like an insult, sitting on a stoop, warning everyone when the police rode by.

"Well, I'm pretty sure if you work hard you'll work your way up," Peace said as he talked about more important matters with Just. Like how they would revenge Assassin s death.

Angella took the time to consult with Terra. While they talked shit about Crook behind his back, he called up, Cherry.

"Sup, ma? What you up to?" "Shopping , why?" She inquired.

"Come pick me up."

"Give me about 15 minutes. I have to pay for these clothes and I'll be on my way," she said.

"Cool." He flipped his cell shut and went to talk to Terra and Angella. "Look, I don't know why y'all tripping. Let's get paid while we can. We got the chance to make some serious money. Are y'all down?" he asked.

"I don't know," Terra stated.

Crook looked at Angella. "You feel the same way?"

"Who wants to get played out, Crook?" she spat.

"Who said I was going to play y'all out? I'm try'na see y'all both sitting on top of the world," Crook sighed. He would hate to lose Angella and Terra because they were two of the best hustlers he ever laid eyes on, but if they chose to leave, then so be it.

"Anyway," spat Terra. "I'll try to be nice to you, but if you give us any crap, we're leaving," she threatened. "Oh, yeah, since we work for you now, maybe you can hit us off with a little spending money. " Terra held out her hand. "You want us representing at our welcome home party tonight, don't you?"

"No doubt. " Crook reached in his pocket and broke them off four thousand in spending money. A small price for two above- average hustlers. "I better see y'all first thing Monday morning. "

Terra smiled as she took the money in her hand. "That's what I'm talking about. Thanks player. " Terra and Angella waved at Crook as they went to go shopping and get ready for their welcome home party at the Sugar Shack later on tonight.

Everyone hustler and so called hustler was at Angella and Terra's homecoming party at the Sugar Shack. Even the F.B.I. and D.E.A. showed up, taking pictures in the parking lot of everyone going in and out of the popular club. Their intentions were to get a feel of who the top notch ballers were. Peace pulled up to the club in his black Maserati with D on the passenger side. Right behind them was Just with his two new girlfriends, India and Irie. A couple of cars back was Crook with his new ride-or-die chick Cherry. Then behind Crook was Malik in his Cadillac Escalade with lil Love and Rico, then behind them was Hot Jit in his Chevy Tahoe. Big Boy in his Lincoln Navigator with Joint that Nigga, Astrop C Rize and Whodie. Murder with Harlem, 45, Big B, Skee, and Nino was cruising dolo.

Inside the club was a couple of well-known people in the point. T.D. a.k.a. Mass Appeal, Polly. A.k.a Street General. Scoobie, Travis, J-sun, Chevy Boy, Kendell, H.P the Great. A.B. Kobe, A.J. Mike Lee, Paul, Eric and Dawarren Crosby. Coby, Jr. Mac, Tellas, Poncho, Pop, Jo-Jo, and Grizz, Wendell and Twin, Terrance, Lacy, Devon Herring, Lucky Lucci, J. DIXON.

***

"Who's those guys?" Special agent Mark Caper asked his partner. Reynolds Travis.

"That's the Q-lnfinity gang, Mark's partner stated while taking pictures.

"Who's their leader?" Mark asked. "Don't know," Reynolds replied.

"Find out. I'm pretty sure they're doing something." Commented Mark.

***

Two thick sisters on all black Suzuki Hayabusa motorcycles pulled up beside Crook's Chrysler 300, parked their bikes and got off.

Crook didn't know his mouth was wide the fuck open and that he was practically drooling on himself until Cherry snapped him out of his wishful thinking.

"Are you going in or what?" she asked.

"Yeah, let me get the door for you," Crook responded as he got out of the car and went to the passenger side to get the door for Cherry. The girl's on the motorbikes took their helmets off and he started giggling.

"Hey, Crook." Terra waved and so did Angella.

"Damn nigga. Are you going to let me out of the car?" Cherry asked with much attitude.

"Sorry. I got you ma." He held the door.

"Yeah, right. What you doing is looking at them heffah's ass's," she snapped as she let herself out the car.

"No I wasn't," he lied.

"Yes you were. I just seen you. You know what, just take me in the club,' she yapped.

"Hey, boss. See you on Monday." Angella waved to piss off the chicken head Crook was with.

"Hey, Crook." Terra flirted in a teasing manner as she and Angella went inside the club in their skin tight leather.

"What was that all about?" Cherry looked at Crook.

"It's nothing," he replied.

"It's better not be. I thought it was all about me?" she commented.

"And it is." He kissed her moist lips and sucked on her bottom lip. "Did I tell you how great you look tonight?" He asked as he wondered about the shit Angella and Terra had just pulled.

Angella and Terra sipped Remy Martin all the while discussing who was cute and who wasn't. "Crook is too cute," Stated Angella. "I swear to Gawd I want to fuck him."

"Yeah. I would probably fuck him too if he wasn't so conceited with his fine ass. And look at that tramp he with," Terra stated.

"That square ass bitch don't have nothing on us." Angella rolled her eyes. "Can't even dance. Let's go show her how to twerk.

Crook was on the dance floor dancing with Cherry when Angella and Terra walked up. "Q-infinity," Angella yelled out as she bent down and slapped her ass with her hand, She smiled, knowing she had Crook's undivided attention. Terra walked up to Angella and they danced erotic with each other, giving Crook a show he would never forget.

"Umm!" Cherry sucked her teeth. "I'll be back," she whispered into Crook's ear. "He's mine," Cherry said to the two queen hoochie mommas dancing close by as she went to the ladies room.

Terra and Angella walked to Crook. Before he had a chance to say a word, Terra started freaking him from behind while Angella freaked him from the front.

"What the fuck!" he said as Terra squeezed his dick with both hands, "Bitch, is you crazy?"

"Shut up." Angella squeezed his ass.

When Cherry returned, the two hoochie mommas had stopped freaking her man. She rolled her eyes. The nerve of these bitches. She paid them little attention. "I got something I think you might want."

"What's that?" he asked curiously.

She gave Crook the panties she had taken off in the bathroom stall and snickered at the two heffah's as she and Crook made their way out of the club and headed for the car.

"That bitch is a straight ho," Terra spat.

"Gosh Crook got a big ass cock." Angella kept it gutter.

"I can't blame that bitch for getting upset. I would've did the same thing!" she giggled. "I gotta get me some of that," She thought about Crook.

"Same here," Terra unconsciously remarked.

"Here I was thinking you hated Crook." Angella took a sip of the Remy from her cup.

"Nah, I don't hate him. I just didn't want him fucking with you cause I would hate to kick that ass."

"You is so wrong for that! To keep things cool between us, neither of us is allowed to fuck with him. Promise," Angella asked.

"Promise. Now let's go find my future baby' s daddy ," said Terra, glimpsing at all the sexy ballers throughout the club.

Peace introduced D to everyone in his clique except for Guns, who for some reason was a no-show. "Yo, hold tight," Peace told D , "I gotta handle a few things."

"Okay ," she replied.

"Don't move," he told her.

"I won't," she smiled as he walked off. As she observed the scene as well as the club, a guy with expensive jewelry approached her. He was accompanied by a beautiful brown-toned lady who appeared to be in her late twenties or early thirties.

"Yo, you Peace's girl, right?" Guns asked.

"Yeah," she replied.

"Keep your eye on her for me," Guns said , leaving Tonya behind.

"Shit," D said to herself.

"This party is pretty live. Can you roll with me to the

ladies room?" Tonya asked.

"I'm waiting for someone," D said as she danced to the music.

"Come on. Peace won't be back for a minute " Tonya said.

"And how do you know that?"

"Cause Guns said he had to talk to Peace about putting Crook in charge when Crook couldn't hustle as good as him. He said Peace had to be out of his rabbit mind ," Tonya yapped.

"This bitch is a blabber mouth," D thought to herself , "What else did he say?"

"I'll tell you in the ladies room. Come on," Tonya said.

When they got in the ladies room, Tonya went into her purse and pulled out a makeup kit with a powdery substance. She took a dollar bill and took a sniff. "You want some?" she asked.

"No." D shook her head from side to side.

"Suit yourself." Tonya did another line.

"So you were saying?" D asked. ·

"Oh yeah. Guns said it wouldn't be long before Peace fucked everything up. Said if it wasn't for him, Peace wouldn't be riding around in all those fly ass whips. Said Peace ain't give a damn about no one but himself. And that soon he wouldn't need Peace."

D crossed her arms and spat, "Is that right." This powder head had to be, dumber than a bag of rocks. "What else did he say?" she asked.

"That Peace was planning something big for those guys who killed Assassin. He didn't know what it was or when it was, but whenever it was, he was getting the hell out of Dodge. I was thinking we could go to Miami, Jamaica, or Brazil. Never been to any one of those places but I would sure like to go. Hold my purse while I use the restroom."

D took Tonya's purse. The things she heard frightened her. She loved Peace and didn't want any harm to come his way.

As D waited for Tonya, two chicken heads walked into the ladies room.

"Girl, them Q-Infinity niggas is all up in here," one said.

"Yeah, them niggas got shit on lock. You know they beefing with those niggas on South Side. I heard it through the grapevine that Cash and his crew killed Assassin. That don't make no damn sense cause that nigga was fine," the other replied.

"You know, right?" one said , giving her girl a high five and laughing.

D couldn't believe her ears. If these two bimbos knew all of this, wasn't no telling who else knew about the situation.

"Y'all two trifling ho's better not let me catch y'all near my man," Tonya spat as she came out of the bathroom stall.

"Umm!" one girl said to the other before leaving out the ladies room.

"Those bitches got no class," Tonya said as if she did. She washed her hands, grabbed her purse, then she and D went to the bar.

"Where you been, ma?" Peace wrapped his arms around D.

"I went to the ladies room." She smiled as Peace kissed her.

"Who this bitch?" Trish tossed her drink at Peace.

D blanked out. Before she knew what happened, she was out of her seat and pouncing on ole girls' ass. "Stupid bitch! How you gone disrespect my man like that?!" Whop-whop! was the sound as D took it to Trish's ass. She went to draw her hand back and was snatched up from behind.

"Let me go!" she protested.

"Fuck her! She not worth it!" Peace held D as she fought to break free.

"Let me beat that bitch ass!" D yelled.

"Come on!" Peace didn't know what got into D, but he grabbed her by the arm and led her out of the club and to his car.

"Let me go! I hate you!" She used her fist and pounded on his chest as tears slid down her eyes.

"What's wrong?" he asked as he pulled her to his chest and hugged her tight, "Tell me what I did wrong?"

"I'm tired, Peace," she cried , "I feel like I'm gonna lose you to the streets."

"Don't cry ma. " Peace lifted her head and kissed her passionately. "It'll be alright. I'll be out the game in a few weeks," he assured her.

"I love you Peace."

"I love you back. " He wiped her tears away and opened the door to the car.

Later on that night, Peace made passionate love to D. She came twice and he came last. As they laid in the bed all hugged up lovey dovey , Peace started to laugh to himself.

"What?" D asked, wondering what was so funny.

"I didn't know you was so nice with those hands or I

would've got you to kick Trish's ass a long time ago."

She giggled and said , "I know a little something but your ex pissed me off tonight. What can I say?" Since they were talking, she decided to turn the conversation in a different direction. "What's up with Guns?" she asked , "He seems shady."

"Why you say that?" He looked over at D.

"Cause I was talking to his girl Tonya. Did you know she's a powder head?"

"No."

"Well, she is. Looks like she's on it pretty bad. "

"Back to Guns," he inquired.

"Well, Tonya was telling me that Guns was pretty pissed off about you putting Crook in charge of things and not him. He feels like he's the reason you riding around in the fly ass rides and shit."

"Oh yeah?" He was shocked by all of this but not surprised.

"Yeah. Guns seems to think you out your rabbit mind for

putting Crook in charge and not him. Tonya's not the brightest bitch in the world. She was telling me that you had something planned for those guys who had something to do with Assassin s death. I don't want you getting in any trouble, Peace," she looked at him and said, "cause I love you so much! "

He kissed D on the forehead and replied , "I love you too." "Then promise me you won't ever leave me," she said as she

rubbed his face.

"For nothing in this world. " He pulled her onto his lap so that she was mounted on top of him. She rode him nice and slow. Their bodies became one as they got lost inside each other.

Chapter 13

"That party was so off the hook Saturday," Terra said to Angella.

"Especially the fight. Peace's girl beat the shit out of Trish. That bitch had it coming," Angella chuckled , "but what's up with you and dark skin Jermaine?"

Terra laughed. "Nothing, but I did meet this guy name C." "What's up with him?" Angella asked.

"I don't know, but this him now." Terra answered her cell. "Hello?" As Terra talked to C, Crook walked into the trap spot. She could see the passion marks across his neck as he took a seat on the sofa.

"Are those hickies on your neck?" Angella asked, taking a seat beside Crook and inspecting his neck. "Umm! Somebody been getting they freak on."

"Mind your business," Crook said.

"You is my business. " She nudged him in the ribs with her elbow. "Terra, ask C if he got some friends?"

"My girl wants to know if you got any friends. He can't be ugly," she warned.

"And he gotta have some money! " Angella yelled out,

"cause I ain't fucking with no broke nigga."

"Can you tell that nigga to call back?" Crook told Terra.

"No," she replied.

Crook went over to Terra and took the phone out of her hand. "Aa-yo. She'll get back at you in a few. She gotta handle some business. " Crook closed the cell, ending the call.

Terra rose from the sofa, placed her hand on her hip and said , "Damn fool! You can't be doing that. You seen me on the phone. "

"Rule number one: no phones," Crook replied.

"The next thing you know he'll have us walking through the house butt naked," Terra whined.

"That might be a good idea," he rubbed his chin and smirked.

"Hell no," Angella disagreed.

"Just kidding. Gosh! Stop being so uptight. Come with me," he said to Angella and Terra. He walked to the courtyard and asked, "Tell me what y'all see." He held his arms out wide and looked at them.

Was this a trick question? Angella thought to herself. "Dope-fiends, crackheads, thirsty ass hustlers," she replied.

"And opportunity. I think if we get watchout men on the rooftops with binoculars and assault rifles, that will eliminate the robberies that's been going on. We also need a spot to count money and one to cook up, then we give the so- called thirsty hustlers their own complex so they won't be out here fighting over sells, ya dig? We have three shifts,

1st, 2nd, and 3rd. Each complex will have one crib from

which they buy from, and the other in which they can smoke and enjoy their high. When our workers run out of product, it's our job to collect and hit them off with more work. Two more things. Actually three. We fall back on Sundays. No one, I mean no one, is to grind on Sundays. Keep the seventh day holy out of respect. God created everything in six days, and on the seventh day, He rested. I want everyone who cops to be patted down thoroughly and frisked. And rule number three. Send out word that if you hustle on our strip you catching a full clip. Y'all feeling that?" he asked.

"I think it's brilliant," Angella responded. "What about you?" he asked Terra.

"It sounds good to me," she had to admit. She just didn't understand where they fitted into the equation.

"Good , cause I'm gonna need y'all to put the word out. I'm gonna also need y'all to collect money, cook, and bag up all of our work in blue vials. That way we can identify our product from the next man's. " Crook left Angella and Terra to handle things.

Weeks had went by and things were going better than ever. "Girl, this is the most money I ever seen in my life." Angella said to Terra as money flipped through the money machine.

"Crook is gonna be so proud of us," Terra stated.

"I know right. He really trust us to leave us around this money and shit," Angella said out of the blue.

"And?" Terra looked at Angella with a sideways glance. "Why wouldn't he?" she asked.

"Cause this a shitload of money," Angella laughed.

Terra laughed her damn self. "You is so stupid," she replied as her cell rung.

"Who is that?" asked Angella.

"C," Terra replied as she flipped open the cell on her hip and answered. "Hey C. Yeah, I missed you."

"When can I see you?" asked C.

She sighed. She really liked C, but had been too busy to get more acquainted with him. "I don't know. I really been so busy lately."

"Damn ma. How about you go to this Usher show with me tonight. I got tickets. You down?"

"What time?" she smiled.

"Seven-thirty tonight," said C.

"Okay. See you then." She hung up and screamed out loud. "Girl! I'm going to see Usher at the Greensboro Coliseum tonight!

Crook walked into the apartment. "What up? Y'all count that money up?" he asked.

"Yeah, we made a hundred thousand this week," Angella said proudly.

"That's what I'm talking about. " Crook took a bunch of hundreds from his pockets, four thousand to be exact. He gave it to Angella. "Yall go and make sure yall extra sexy tonight. I'm taking y'all out."

"I can't. " Terra frowned up.

This ungrateful bitch, Crook thought. "And why not?" he asked.

"Cause I'm going out with C." She sucked her teeth at him.

"Call that nigga and tell him you can't make it," he said.

"You can't be serious," she said to him. Who was he to think he could control me. I'm Terra. The Boss chick.

"Dead serious," said Crook, "Get on the phone and tell that nigga you can't make it."

"I'm going ," Terra stood up from the sofa and mouthed off. Before she knew what happened , Cook got up from the sofa and smacked the daylights out of her. His hand gripped around her throat, making it impossible to breathe.

"Stop, Crook!" Angella pleaded.

"Shut the fuck up!" he barked. He commenced to choking Terra until he was good and ready and let her fall to the floor. "I'm tired of you thinking you run shit. I'm tired of you always wearing jeans and white-T's. Bitch, you a lady so I want you dressing classy from now on." He walked up to her and lifted her face up. "And do something about your hair. It's fucked up."

"Fuck you!" Terra spat.

"No, fuck wit' me," he said before leaving.

"I hate him," Terra said , "I'm going to that show tonight." She wiped her tears away.

"I hate to say this, but you can be a bitch sometimes." Angella kept it real.

"He didn't have to put his hands on me."

"Yeah , but you have to know that men have a thing called ego. Look on the bright side. This nigga gave us four thousand so let's make the best out of it." Angella helped Terra off the ground.

Crook knew he was wrong for choking Terra out, but word up, he had got jealous for some reason. He called up Angella.

"Hello." She answered on the first ring.

"What's good?"

"We getting our hair done."

"Terra still mad at me?" he asked.

"You know she is but she'll get over it. You re gonna love her new look."

"What about yours?" asked Crook, "You gonna look good for me?"

"Of course," she replied , " Wait until you see me."

"I can't." He laughed , flirting a little. "So why was Terra so upset?"

Angella looked over at Terra as she got her hair done. Crook was really on Terra as of lately. She had to make sure to look extra scrumptious for him tonight to make Crook notice her. "She really wanted to go see Usher tonight."

"Usher or C?" he asked.

"Usher." Angella chuckled. "But like I said , she'll get over it."

"Right," said Crook.

"So where are you?" Angella asked.

"Riding around. About to go check on my suit and then come and pick yall up."

"You wearing a suit?" Angella asked in disbelief.

"Yeah."

"I can't believe it."

"Why not?" he shot back.

"Cause, I never had you wearing a suit. I bet you'll look nice though." She smiled.

"You flirting?"

"A little bit." She blushed until she caught Terra ice grilling her. "Let me get off this phone so I can finish getting my hair done."

"Aight." Crook laughed as he got off the phone and fired up his blunt. Ever since the night Angella and Terra had freaked him on the dance floor, he had been wanting them. Crook had went and got his suit tailored. After getting fresh to death, he went to go check on the limo. Five minutes before seven that night, he pulled in front of the projects for all to see.

"Damn girl. It's a limo outside." Angella told Terra.

"Let me see," Terra took a look out the blinds.

"My cell is ringing." Angella ran to her cell. "Hello." she answered excited.

"Come outside. Can't you see I'm waiting on you two?" Crook was outside the limo staring at his Rolex.

"We're coming," Angella said, grabbing her purse. "Come on," she replied to Terra.

Crook stood outside the limo being admired by all when Angella and Terra came out looking good as ever. Angella wore a strapless dress by Christian Dior and black stiletto heels, her long wavy locks hung freely down her back. Just what a nigga needed. Something to pull on, he thought. She was drop-dead gorgeous like she told him she would be, but it was Terra who got his dick hard the minute he saw her. He was lost for words. She wore a skimpy black dress that left the mind wondering.

"Y'all look beautiful," he said as he held the door for them to get in the limo.

Angella smiled. "You too, handsome. "

"I'm still mad at you," Terra gritted. Crook was looking all too sexy. He was wearing a white and black pinstriped Armani suit, black dress shirt and brim hat like that of a mob boss.

"Where we going?" asked Angella.

"Just sit back and see," said Crook as he climbed into the backseat of the limo with the girls.

Terra watched Angella throw herself all on Crook. And what about the promise we made not to fuck him, Terra thought as Crook rubbed Angella's backside. Not that she was jealous of her girl, cause Angella was stunning, but she had went way out of her element to make him happy. She had gotten girly girly, gotten her hair pressed , nails and toes did , and had even threw on a lousy dress, which she hated , and here he was rubbing on Angella. Terra was willing to bet any amount of money that if she had not been in the limo, Crook and Angella would be getting it in.

"You aight Ma?" Crook asked , sensing something was wrong with Terra.

"I guess. Just don't wanna be here," she said.

"You probably need a drink.' Crook opened the cooler and pulled out a large bottle of Hennessy. He poured them a drink , himself one, and then sparked a blunt the size of a miniature baseball bat. By the time they got to downtown Charlotte, they were lifted. The limo pulled up to a club called Vibrations Night Lounge.

The limo driver opened the door and waited for them to exit the limo. "This place is packed ," Angella said as she looked around , "It's going to take forever for us to get inside."

Crook got on his cell and called a dear friend. Minutes later they were inside the lounge, being escorted to a reserved table close to the stage.

"Let me get a couple bottles of Cristal for the sexy ladies," Crook said to the waitress as they took a seat at their table.

"Anything else?" asked the waitress.

"Yeah, let us get the jerk chicken, fried rice, cornbread , and sweet potatoes," Crook said.

"And what about dessert?" the waitress asked.

"Strawberry cheesecake," he replied.

"Alright. Enjoy yourselves. Be back in a few," said the waitress as she walked off.

Terra would be telling a lie if she said she didn't have the best time of her life. Crook had went all out. How about they got to see performers such as Brian McKnight, Anthony Hamilton, and the singer Joe. She enjoyed all the performers, but Joe the most. Especially when he performed the classic hit, "Things Your Man Want Do."

"So did y'all have a good time?" Crook asked as he led the ladies to the limo.

"It was okay ," Terra replied.

"I had a good time bae." Angella placed her arm in Crook's arm and rested her head on his broad shoulder as they walked to the limo, then replied , "It was better than that stupid Usher concert. "

Terra sucked her teeth. Look at this bitch getting fly out the mouth. As they approached the limo and got in, her cell began to ring. "Hello," she answered, and smiled once she heard C's voice.

Crook sat across from Terra as Angella kissed on his neck and gently grabbed his crotch. He stared at Terra as she talked to C. It's like the nigga had some kind of hold on her or something. Terra was a valuable asset to him, as well as Angella, and he didn't need nothing or no one coming in the middle of that. He knew Angella was loyal and would do as he asked, but this bitch Terra was a whole nother story.

"I'm on my way home now. You wanna come over. Alright, hit me back later then." She ended the call.

"Umm! C gonna bang that shit up tonight," Angella said. Terra could be so stupid. This would definitely fuck up her chances with Crook, she thought. "Drop her off and let's go to my place," she whispered into Crook's ear.

Crook noticed Terra hadn't said two words the whole ride back to the Point. He was disappointed after all the trouble he went through getting the tickets, not to mention the limo.

"Yo! Take me to Lake View Apartments," Crook told the driver.

When they pulled up to Angella's apartment, Crook got out and walked her to the door.

"Well, this is it," she said.

"Yeah," Crook said , "I really need to be getting back to the spot."

"You can't come in for a minute?" she asked.

"Nah, maybe we can kick it tomorrow," he told her.

"Promise." Angella leaned forward and kissed him slow but passionately. "Too bad you couldn't stay," she said before going into her apartment.

"Where to?" the limo driver asked Crook as he got back into the limo. "Ambassador Court. " Crook leaned back in his seat. Once again Terra was on her cell talking to C.

"I'll be home in a few. Yeah. I don't mind if you stop by after you leave the Waffle House." Terra finished her call and flipped her cell shut.

"I need to use the bathroom. Can I come up?" Crook asked as the limo driver pulled up to Terra's complex.

"No, piss on yourself ," she spat.

"Come on," he begged , "I gotta piss like a racehorse. "

"Piss outside," she said.

"What about your neighbors?"

She laughed. "They won't laugh at how small you are," she said as she got out of the limo.

"Let me walk you to the door."

"No thank you. I can manage," she spat.

"Hold up." He yanked her by the arm and disregarded anything she had to say. "I hate that funky attitude."

"So, I hate you more. I told you I can manage. " She tried getting out of his masculine grip.

"Yo, give me a minute," he told the limo driver as he forcefully lead Terra to her apartment. "Why you so damn mean, gosh, I only gotta use the bathroom. " He gripped his genitals and hobbled from one leg to the other. "Come on wit' your mean ass. We supposed to be clique."

"You should've thought about that when you put your hands on me. " She opened the door and let him in.

"Where to?" he asked , hobbling from side to side. "Second door down the hall," she said.

"Damn!" Crook rushed to the bathroom, called the limo

driver and told him he could leave, then took a piss.

Terra took a peek out the window to see if C had pulled up when she noticed the limo driver pulling off. "Crook!" she yelled out.

"Yo! What up, ma?" he asked as he stepped out of the bathroom.

"You better call that limo driver back cause he just pulled off.

"Word." He looked out the window.

"That's bullshit! You know I m about to have company. You want me to call you a cab?" she asked.

"Nah, I'll sit tight." He sat down on the sofa and made himself at home.

"Oh , Hell-nah! You gotta leave," she stated , "C should be here at any moment ."

"Who the fuck is this nigga C, and how long you been talking to this nigga?" he asked as he sparked up a blunt he had in his front pocket.

"None of your business. You want me to call you a cab so you can bounce?" she asked for the second time.

"No cause I ain't leaving ," he said arrogantly.

"Shit," she said out loud. Then she heard a horn blow. It was C. "I can't believe you doing this." She panicked. What was she going to tell C? She should've never let this crazy ass nigga in her freaking house.

There was a knock on the door. Crook pulled out his 45 and walked up to her. "Tell him to bounce before he catch a cap in his ass." He cocked the hammer to his gun. "You better talk to him before I do. It's just me and you tonight. " He scanned his finger down her arm to her curvaceous hips and laughed.

"Stupid ass nigga." She walked to the door, put the chain on the latch and cracked the door slightly.

"Sup, ma. Smell like you up in there blazing. Let me in," said C.

"I'm sleeping," she lied. "Stop," she said to Crook as he pressed up against her.

C was confused. "What? Stop playing. You told me to come by."

"I lied ," she said, trying her best to shove Crook away from the door.

"She busy you lame ass nigga," Crook spat, "Get lost." He unlatched the door so C could see him hugged up against Terra.

"You a day late and a dollar short." Crook kissed Terra on her neck. "Get the fuck outta here," he spat as he revealed his chrome 45 in his right hand.

"I'm sorry C," she apologized.

"You should be. All you had to do was tell me you had a man and I would've never came here. You a bad bitch but I ain't try'na die for it." C held up his hands in submission.

"Sorry player," he apologized.

"Ain't no love lost," Crook said as he wrapped his arm around Terra.

"Crook, why did you do that?" she shouted.

"Fuck that nigga," he said arrogantly.

"You need to leave," she fussed, "I hate you."

"Do you?" He pulled her up against him and kissed her lips softly.

"What are you doing?" she pleaded.

Crook scooped her up and used the wall to prop her up against. "Damn I been waiting to do this for a long time."

"Likewise," she agreed , kissing his lips and placing her arms around his neck.

"Damn you smell good , and you look so sexy with your hair down. See how bad I want you?" He placed her hand up against his brick-hard dick. "I'm about to tear that pussy up." He eased her to the sofa. She was taking control. "Stop fighting me. "

"Sorry," she moaned , arching her back in submission.

Crook laid her down on the sofa, straddled her, and hiked up the dress she had on. He then slid her undergarments to the side and stuck one finger inside of her warmth , then two fingers. "Damn I'm lucky." He pulled his two fingers out, tasted her juices, then replaced his fingers with his face.

She guided his head as he ate her out. "Crook, Crook," she called out as her chest heaved in, "That feels so good." She gyrated her hips. "Don't stop," she pleaded.

Crook's tongue flickered as Terra called out his name on numerous occasions. He licked all around her pussy lips until at last her body shook and she came on his face.

He pulled down his pants and took Terra right there on the couch. "Tell me this me right here. " He plowed in and out of her missionary style.

"Yes baby it's yours! " She gripped his ass as he dove in and out of her deeply until at last, he went limp and collapsed on top of her. They were both panting and breathing from the lovemaking.

"Damn your clothes are sweaty. I got a shower and some

extra clothes in my room," she said , "Come on." She grabbed him by the hand and led him to her room, where they got undressed and got into the shower. Once in, Crook rammed into her from the back while caressing her C-cup breast. They weren't too small but yet a handful. He sucked one as he drove in her with long, agile strokes.

After great sex, they laid in bed hugged up. Terra rubbed Crook's chest gently and said, "I hate I was so mean to you."

"Same here," he said as he took a puff from his blunt.

"So what now? You go back to your girl and I go back to being alone. " She kissed his nipples, teasing his areolas. "So you think I fucked you just to fuck you?" he asked.

"I mean…" She shrugged. "You was all on my girl tonight."

He smiled. "You mean she was on me. "

"Yeah, whatever. So what made you want to kick it with me tonight?" she asked.

"Come here." He pulled her out of bed. As they stood in front of her bedroom mirror, he said, "Tell me what you see."

"Me naked," she giggled.

"That too," he teased.

She laughed and asked, "What else?"

"I see a shorty who will ride or die for me, in you I see loyalty and determination. You my very own dime piece. " He hugged her.

"You think I'm a dime piece? She gazed back at him.

"Ain't no question." He nibbled on her shoulder. "My dime piece."

"So I'm your dime piece?" she asked with sarcasm.

"For sure. But you gon' have to start listening to me and trust I wouldn't do anything to hurt you. You need to stop fighting with me, and make sure these snakes don't fuck up this thing of ours. You got my back." He asked.

***

"Something sure wasn't right." Thought Angella as she stared at Terra and then Crook. It was obvious something happened last night. She got up from the sofa and walked over to Terra. "So what happened to your neck?" She inspected closely.

"You nosy as shit! Stay out of my business." Terra smiled in Crooks direction. She could see him grinning as he read the High Point Enterprise.

"Since when did we start keeping secrets?" Angella asked, glimpsing up and catching how Terra and Crook made constant eye contact. She put the pieces to the puzzle together. "So you broke our promise as well as our friendship?" She gritted between clenched teeth.

"Crook did y'all fuck!" Angella asked him.

"Is you crazy? Terra can't stand me." He replied.

"You better not be lying. Cause if you are, I promise I will fuck the both of you up." She threatened.

"Ain't nobody doing what you think." Terra rolled her eyes.

"Better not be, cause If I find out, it's on, believe that." Spat Angella as she glared at Terra with suspicion.

***

Peace pulled up to the projects in his Range Rover and waited on Crook to bring the drop off to him. When Crook hopped into the Range Rover Peace could see he had some heavy shit on the brain. "What's wrong."

"Just waiting for you to come back." Crook gave Peace the book bag of money. In return Peace gave Crook a book bag filled with raw coke. "Don't worry, you got everything handled." Peace gave his young lion the confidence he needed.

"I know but shit ain't the same without you nigga. Instead of you and Assassin. It's Angella and Terra."

Peace laughed. Crook looked at him. "What's so funny?" Crook asked.

"Nothing. I just thought you would've fucked them both by now. That's why I set things up the way I did. What's taking you so long." Peace asked.

"I don't know. I'm kinda feeling Terra." He stated. "You know what I'm saying?"

"And Angella?" Peace questioned.

"She tripping right now. If she find out about me and Terra she might spazz out. She a major asset to the team and I would hate to lose her over some bullshit." Crook sighed.

Peace understood where Crook was coming from. "Do what you gotta do to keep her on your good side. Spend some one on one time with her, take her out, kiss her, do something nigga, but don't fuck up what we got going on right here." Peace glimpsed down at the book bag with the money in it.

"Facts," Replied Crook as he nodded his head in agreement.

"So everything good?" Peace wanted to know.

"Cool. Everybody eating good, niggas know not to hustle nowhere near this motherfucker or it's murder," Crook smiled his arrogant smile.

"Good. And remember to do what you have to do to keep Terra and Angella happy so we can continue to get this money."

"Right." Crook was about to get up out the ride when he remembered something that had been on his mind. "Yo. When we gon' get at them little South Side niggas?"

"In due time." Replied Peace. Little did Crook know but he had his team of assassins on the hunt as he spoke.

***

Chip smacked the shit out a dope-fiend that had been owing him money for the last two weeks. "Get the fuck up outta here." Said Chip. As everyone laughed and stared at the situation. Two dark Tahoe's with tinted windows rolled up on the scene. At first Chip thought it was undercovers, but when shots rang out he didn't have time to react or grab his gun. It's like his feet were stuck to the pavement. Had he reached his fate? He thought as a stray bullet blew the top of his head off.

Big boy, Hot Jit, Murder, Skee Mask, Joint, and Billie Joe jumped out of the SUV's and started blasting away. They didn't care who they killed and wanted to make the cats from the Southside endure the pain they had been going through with losing Assassin. Milk, Lil Love, Rico,

Tyshawn, TD, and Qwest jumped out of the second vehicle and started blasting away. The Q-Infinity click murdered as many as they could before hopping back into their vehicles and speeding off.

***

Somewhere in Winston Salem, NC. In a Holiday Inn, Cash laid on the bed as Trish rode him like a tsunami wave.

***

"This shit was better than I could've imagined," Bear remarked as him and 45 sat in a black Yukon Denali with Binoculars peeking into Cash's hotel room as Trish bounced up and down on his dick.

"Let me see," 45 reached for the binoculars.

"Hold up, son." Bear laughed.

"Fuck that." 45 took the binoculars from Bear and took a look at the peek show. "This shit better than that Ray J and Kim Kardashian shit! I know Peace ain't gon' kill this bitch!" 45 stated distastefully.

"The hell he ain't." Stated bear snatching the binoculars. It was time to go to work. "You ready?" Bear asked.

"Let's do it." Replied 45.

The two men took the steps and made sure the coast was clear before tapping on Cash's room door.

"Damn! Who is that?" Trish glimpsed at the door as she rode the fuck out of Cash's dick.

"What now?" Cash asked out loud. "Who is it?"

"Room Service."

Before Cash had time to grab his gun from the counter, he was gazing down a black hole. "Don't kill me," He pleaded.

"I won t. But Peace will. Tie this bamma up." Bear said to 45.

The last thing Cash remembered was a gun cracking him across the head and then waking up in a cold abandoned warehouse. "What the fuck." He asked. His vision was blury like he was in the Twilight Zone. He could see three figures but his vision was to fuzzy to make them out.

Peace walked up to Cash and tapped him on the face. "Wake up rapist." He spit in Cash's face. "So you killed my homie and fucked my bitch?" He looked over at Trish who was tied in a chair opposite from Cash.

"We wasn't fucking, Peace." She shouted. "I love you Peace."

"Please bitch. I got love for you too. Come on girls." Peace waved Angella and Terra into the room. "Assassin told me I should've had this done a long time ago. Give her a face lift."

"No. Trish screamed before she was given a buck fifty across her face. What use to be beauty was now a soggy mess and a memory of what use to be a bad bitch.

"Kill her." Peace closed his eyes as Terra sliced the main artery in Trish's neck.

Cash puked all over his fresh Jordan's. "Don't kill me." He shouted.

"Shut up, bitch." Peace lifted Cash's head up so he could look into his eyes. "You killed my motherfucking homie."

he spazzed out and started beating Cash like a heavyweight boxer until he knocked both Cash and the chair on the ground.

He waited ten minutes for Cash to regain consciousness then asked Bear to go get the bag of double D batteries from the car.

"What you need batteries for," Bear asked. "Just go get them." Peace shouted.

Bear left and came back with grocery bags filled with double D batteries. He sat the bag down on the unsteady table for Peace. "Here they go."

"Good looking," remarked Peace. Then he started unwrapping the packs of batteries a pack at a time. He unwrapped as many as he could and then started tossing them upside Cash's head until he had numerous speed knots and looked like Wile E. Coyote. "What you kill'em for?" Peace shouted.

"I didn't. Guns did." Cash moaned out in pain.

"I don't believe you. You lying piece of shit!" he threw another battery that bust Cash upside his head. "Stop lying to me."

"It's the truth. You got the wrong guy. How could I kill Assassin when I jumped off the roof? It was Guns who pushed him off the roof." As blood dripped from his face, he could see the hurt and deceit in Peace's eyes. He used the opportunity to show Peace what type of crud-ball he was dealing with. "Believe me man. You can let me go and we can forget this whole thing happened. I was thinking we could link up and get this money. I'm tired of buying coke from Guns anyway." He could see Peace was having a hard time deciphering what he just heard.

"This is just one big mistake." He said as he started choking on his own blood.

"You right. Take him up out of here and get him something to drink." Peace said to Bear and 45.

"Oh shit!" Angella thought. She had just remembered that Guns was supposed to meet Crook at the spot in a few minutes. She pulled out her cell and dialed Crooks number while running to her motorcycle.

Angella sped through traffic and ran red lights to get to the spot in a timely manner.

"Sup nigga?" Crook opened the door for Guns. "Let me go grab that for you?"

"Word," Guns grinned. "You here by yourself?"

"Yeah. Let me go get that. Have a seat." He told Guns. He had a funny feeling. Something told him not to make this transaction. Crook went into the backroom where he kept all the work at. What was up with that grin? Crook always went with his instinct so he wasn't about to change up now. His cell rang. He answered.

"Get out the house. Guns killed Assassin." Angella said as she ran up the steps, damn she wished they hadn't broken the elevator system.

Guns sat on the sofa with his hands in his hoody clinching his 9mm. Crook was one dead son-of-a-bitch. Bring that coke out here nigga. He was silently thinking. "Come on," Guns yelled impatiently.

'Tm here already." Crook said as he aimed his 9mm assault rifle in Guns direction.

"Oh shit!" Guns did some fast thinking and let off a shot

to Crooks chest then leaped over the couch as shots rang out. He shot his gun with a sideways aim until he heard Crook whine out in pain. That gave him enough time to make a dash for it. With every step he took there was a shot that followed. He could feel the nearness of the gun blaze as he dove out of the window and onto the fire escape.

Angella shot the lock on the door and disregarded using her key. She kicked the door open and saw Crook sprawled out on the floor. "No baby. Don't you die on me. Don't leave me, bae." She said as she held him in her arms.

***

He ain't get a dime but at least he got up out of there! Something wasn't right. He could feel it in the air when Crook was taking his time in the backroom. "The nigga was probably dying from chest pains, "Guns thought as he dialed Tonya's number on his cell.

She answered, "What up, bae?"

"Pack that money and coke up. We're about to get the fuck out of dodge! Hurry up. I'll be there in about ten minutes."

***

"Crook! Don't die on me!" Angella wept.

Peace and Terra made their way inside the trap spot. First Assassin and now this! Thought Peace. He kept hearing his uncle Roberto s voice in the back of his mind saying. "It's good to have a click in your line of work, but always go with your heart." His uncle had been right. Guns had crossed him over. He had failed as the man who everyone depended on. If it hadn't been for him, Assassin would still be alive, Crook wouldn't be dead on the floor, Yolonda would've have gotten raped and none of this shit would've happened. He sighed. Guess he should've reminded himself to Always Stay On Point.

"Yo. Where we going?" Cash asked.

"We ain't going nowhere but you are." Bear stated as he pulled over on the side of the Yakin River bridge. "Get that nigga the fuck out of the Jeep." Bear told 45 who was in the backseat holding a gun to Cash's rib cage.

"Come on fool!" 45 spat dragging Cash out of the SUV in handcuffs.

"I thought we were going to get drinks?" Cash questioned as he was being dragged against his own will.

"Drinks on me." 45 tossed Cash over the bridge and watched his body tumble to a large body of water.

Conclusion

Whatever happened to the Q-infinity gang? Well. Peace is still doing his thing and seriously thinking about making an exit out the business and settling down with his girlfriend D. Angella and Terra are still holding down the fort like Crook was still around pushing them to get all the money that had yet to be made. Yolanda and Cherry are back to their old ways. Sticking niggas up. Sugar gave birth to a beautiful baby girl named, Ashanti, and is going to school. She even let Assassin's mom Lily move in with her so she could watch Ashanti while she went back school to become a cosmetologist, Officer Wolf can still be found hanging around Irving projects shaking down and harassing the Q-infinity gang.

Stay tuned for the sequel: Always On Point!

1. Who was your favorite Character. Assassin, Crook, Yolonda. Sugar, Cherry, Peace, Just, Trish, D, Terra, Angella, Officer Wolf, Guns, Goldshay, Roberto, Cash, Chip?
2. Follow me on social Media. Devon Wilfoung@ Facebook.com/lnstgram get_on_point.

ABOUT THE AUTHOR

Devon Wilfoung is originally from High Pointe, NC. He is thirty-five years old, has one son, and loves to write, travel and inspire others.

Order Form

MAKE CHECKS AND MONEY ORDERS PAYABLE TO:

Name:____

Address:______________________________________

City:________________ State:________________
Zip:________________

Amount		Book Title or Pen Pal Number	Price
		Included for shipping for 1 book	$4 U.S. / $9 Inter

This book can also be purchased on:
AMAZON.COM/ BARNES&NOBLE.COM/ CREATESPACE.COM